BRADBURY SPEAKS

Too Soon from the Cave,

Too Far from the Stars

RAY BRADBURY

HARPER ● PERENNIAL

NEW YORK ● LONDON ● TORONTO ● SYDNEY

With love to my friends

Loren Eiseley and Aldous Huxley,

whose essays showed me the way

HARPER ● PERENNIAL

Pages 241–43 constitute an extension of this copyright page.

A hardcover edition of this book was published in 2005 by William Morrow, an imprint of HarperCollins Publishers.

FIRST HARPER PERENNIAL EDITION PUBLISHED 2006.

Designed by Fritz Metsch

The Library of Congress has catalogued the hardcover edition as follows:

Bradbury, Ray.
    Bradbury speaks : too soon from the cave,
    too far from the stars / Ray Bradbury.—1st ed.
      p. cm.
    ISBN 0-06-058568-4 (alk. paper)
    1. Title: Too soon from the cave, too far from the stars. II. Title.

PS3503.R167B73 2005
813'.54—dc22   2005041489

ISBN-10: 0-06-058569-2 (pbk.)
ISBN-13: 978-0-06-058569-3 (pbk.)

06 07 08 09 10 ❖/RRD 10 9 8 7 6 5 4 3 2 1

CONTENTS

About Life

About Paris

About Los Angeles

INTRODUCTION

Although I suppose I am best known to readers as a fiction writer, I am also a great lover of the essay and have written hundreds of them. Everyone has heard of the "familiar essay," in which the writer draws on personal life experience, ideas, and the world around him. But few know the term "*unfamiliar* essay," where a god-awful amount of research has to be sweated through. All of the pieces in this book are familiar essays. I've written only one unfamiliar piece; although it is not included here, my experience with it is worth noting.

Some years back, *Life* magazine asked me to write about life on other worlds. In the course of my research, I collected hundreds of pages and dozens of tapes, all of which I dutifully studied, all of which drove me mad with details. I digested all these facts and tried to spit them out again in a piece called "Life on Other Worlds," which I duly mailed off to the magazine.

Deeply displeased with my article, *Life* flew an editor to Los Angeles with scissors and paste to tear my article apart and put it back together. It was ultimately published, but it was dreadful—unfamiliar—work, and as a result is the least favorite of all the essays I've ever written.

All of my other essays were born of explosions of love and quiet passion.

For instance, at lunch with a number of *Life* editors some thirty years ago, I expressed my wild enthusiasm for trains.

"My God," they said. "Why don't you write an article on trains for us?"

"Wait here!" I cried, and ran across the street to my office, where I wrote the piece in a white-hot burst of love and returned to the luncheon table in thirty minutes. I sold the article during dessert.

If you read "Any Friend of Trains Is a Friend of Mine," you can feel the difference between research that one commits in agony and the research of memory and love, which is the finest and the best.

The most successful of my declamatory essays is "The Ardent Blasphemers," where I compare Melville's mad Captain Ahab with Jules Verne's saner Captain Nemo, viewing the dark of one as against the light of the other. My essay shows Ahab daring God to strike him, whereas Nemo plugs into the energy of the universe and ignites the seas.

Two years after this essay was published, two strangers knocked at my door, representing the United States Pavilion to be built for the 1964 New York World's Fair.

"We've come," they said, "to give you a fifty-million-dollar building."

"Come in, come in!" I cried. "What's this?"

"We've read your essay 'The Ardent Blasphemers,'" they said, "describing the gap between crazed Ahab and the mild lunatic Nemo, and their creative blasphemy. It has convinced us that you are the proper one to plan the American Adventure in the United States Pavilion. Can you write a sixteen-minute-long script, accompanied by a full symphony orchestra?"

"I can!" I cried, and did.

So by committing myself to the passionately dramatic, by jumping in headlong and not agonizing over research, my life was changed yet again.

Since then, I've written essays only when they wake me at dawn and ask to be finished by noon.

Thirty-seven of those insistent, wake-me-at-dawn friends are included here. I had great fun poking through my files, pulling these essays out, dusting them off, re-meeting them. Some have been published; I have provided original publication dates for those. The others were written at various times over the years and, I'm afraid, I cannot remember their birthdays, and so they've been annotated as "undated." In some of these undated essays, one can find hints as to the approximate time period in which they were probably written. For example, "I'm Mad As Hell, and I'm Not Going to Take It Anymore!" is undated, but I must have written it in 1999, given the content of the piece. (On another note, it's interesting to observe that in this essay, I refer to the videocassette as a "newborn vaudevillian." Of course, if I wrote the essay today, I would probably refer to the DVD, which was introduced in the late 1990s, and not yet as ubiquitous as it is today.)

"Lord Russell and the Pipsqueak" is a panicked remembrance of my visiting Bertrand Russell and wondering just what in hell I could possibly say to the world's greatest philosopher. Somehow I managed.

"The Affluence of Despair: America Through the Looking Glass" and "Beyond 1984" are rooted in my short story "The Toynbee Convector." Surrounded for years by people who arose each morning on the dark side of their beds, I knew they looked upon me as a fool; I knew otherwise and wrote these two essays because I figured we—our country—would succeed far beyond our wildest dreams and ultimately solve most of our problems if only we kept looking forward, with hope. If you read these essays along with my piece on writing, "My Demon, Not Afraid of Happiness," you will find my soul's blueprint.

In my later years, I have looked in the mirror each day and found a happy person staring back. Occasionally I wonder why I can be so happy. The answer is that every day of my life I've worked only for myself and for the joy that comes from writing and creating. The image in my mirror is not optimistic, but the result of optimal behavior.

Another of my life's loves is France, particularly Paris, City of Light. On my way to Rome fifty years ago, my friend Lord Kilbracken urged me to have dinner in Paris, even though I had only ninety minutes between trains. I obeyed, had dinner, and almost missed my train connection south. From this came "The Sixty-Minute Louvre: Paris by Stopwatch."

"Paris: Always Destroyed, Always Triumphant" concerns the revolutionary history of France compared to the reality of the most beautiful country and the most beautiful city in the world. The ironic difference between the real aesthetic and beautiful France and its political failures during two hundred years is amazing; I could not but write about it.

And, of course, I love my home city of Los Angeles. "L.A., How Do I Love Thee?" and "L.A., Outta the Way and Let Us Happen!" were written because so much of the rest of the country, particularly New York City, has beaten up on us over the years. The great thing about L.A., as indicated in the essays, is that there you have the freedom and opportunity and resources to find your way to become anyone you want. You don't have to assume the attitudes or opinions of the rest of the country. There you find the delicious freedom, especially, to become the kind of writer you want to become.

"Mars: Too Soon from the Cave, Too Far from the Stars" positions us exactly where I think we are at this time in history. We have much to forgive ourselves for, and it all must be forgiven if we are to move forward. Those of us living now are, in my opinion anyway, the in-between generation. It's been only a few thousand years since we emerged from our caves. We have to be patient with ourselves as we move on in our return to the Moon and onward to Mars. I think this is inevitable; it will happen, and we must not let our prejudices stand in our way.

On that final note, dear readers, I leave these familiar essays in your gentle hands.

ABOUT WRITING

MY DEMON, NOT AFRAID
OF HAPPINESS (UNDATED)

I have a strange and incredible muse that, unseen, has engulfed me during my lifetime. I have renamed my muse. In a Frederick Seidel poem, I found a perfect replacement, where he tells of "A Demon not afraid of happiness."

This perfectly describes the Demon that sits now on one shoulder, now on the other, and whispers things that no one else hears.

My Demon warned me one night years ago when I saw some glum theater at UCLA. Later I said to the director, "You want me to stick my wet finger in a wall socket for electrocution. Instead I will screw a brighter bulb in the same socket and light the room."

So my Demon warned me off such encounters and provided invisible material for my future life.

Dandelion Wine, for example, began as an essay in *Gourmet* magazine in 1953, and over the years my Demon tripped me, sprawling, into a novel to be read in American schools.

On my twenty-fourth birthday, I discovered *Winesburg, Ohio*, which is indeed not a novel but a short-story collection by Sherwood Anderson. How fine, I thought, if someday I could birth similar grotesques to inhabit Mars.

My Demon, provoked, secretly made travel plans to landfall Mars, live there, and arrive at an unplanned novel, *The Martian Chronicles*.

Green Shadows, White Whale resulted from my life in Ireland, when for eight months I wrote the screenplay of *Moby Dick* for John Huston. At the time I thought I was not sponging in any of the green atmosphere or the characters of sad and beautiful Ireland. But then one night, a year later, a voice spoke in my head and said, "Ray, darlin'." And I said, "Who's that?" The voice said, "It's Nick, your cabdriver. Remember all those nights of my driving you back from Kilcock to Dublin and describing the mist and the fog and the rain along the way? Do you remember that, Ray?" "Yes," I said. Then the voice said with the voice of my Demon, "Would you get up and put that down?" I got up, surprised, and went to my typewriter and began to write a series of poems, essays, and one-act plays that finally shared a San Francisco theater with Sean O'Casey.

Twenty years passed with more essays, poems, and stories, and I woke one morn to find in that litter *Green Shadows, White Whale*, a novel, complete and intact.

A short tale, "The Black Ferris," melded itself into a screenplay for Gene Kelly, and when Kelly couldn't find the money for the film, I spent three years turning the screenplay into the novel *Something Wicked This Way Comes.*

Then at last there is my late-on offspring *From the Dust Returned*, commenced when I drew skeletons, age six, to scare my cousins, continued in secret when I helped redecorate my grandparents' house with Halloween broomsticks, and ended with a gothic story, "Homecoming," rejected by *Weird Tales* as needful of Marley's ghost and lacking Poe. I sold the story to *Mademoiselle*, and over the years it grew in rain and mist and arrived in fogs as a novel just last year.

What we have here, then, is a very unusual approach to writing and discovering, not knowing the outcome. To move ahead on a blind journey, running fast, putting down thoughts as they occur.

And along the way my inner voice advised:

If you must write of assassinations, rapes, and Ophelia suicides, speak the speech, I pray thee, poetry in your breath, metaphors on your tongue. Remember how glad Iago was to think on Othello's fall. How, with smiles, Hamlet prepared his uncle's death.

Shakespeare and my Demon schooled me so: Be not afraid of happiness. It is often the soul of murder.

VIN REVIVERE,
OR
A VINTAGE REVISITED (1991)

Little did I know, as the old saying goes, that when publishing my "Dandelion Wine" story in *Gourmet* in 1953, I was starting a novel.

The history of my books is most strange. My stories, essays, and poems suddenly grow full and tall.

The Martian Chronicles, for example, born in 1944 as a collection of stories, along the way civilized an entire planet.

Similarly *Green Shadows, White Whale*. My life in Ireland, written as poems and plays, finally became a novel about John Huston and Moby Dick.

"Dandelion Wine," then, was a series of word associations about my hometown, remembering how it was to run in a new pair of tennis shoes or to perch on the family porch on those wonderful summer nights when we filled the sky with rockets and fire balloons.

The novel was published in 1957. Since then I've been astounded to receive letters from Sweden, where summer lasts perhaps three or four days, or Kenya, where summer lasts forever. Then Tokyo. Where is there room for grass anywhere in Tokyo? How in hell could they grow dandelions to make wine?

But every Christmas for twenty years, forty Japanese students air-mail me essays, poems, and novel fragments about *Dandelion Wine* as a special gift to end the year. Their exquisite writing cracks my heart. How peculiar that my grandfather's cellar pressings would be a proper vintage for those Orient students halfway round the world.

Along the way the book has shifted locales and costumed itself in stage plays and musicals. Three different composers have written music for the productions that have appeared in Chicago, Washington, D.C., and Los Angeles.

In my pantry at this moment sit nine bottles of dandelion wine, arrived from every continent. The bottle I treasure most was made from flowers on my grandparents' lawn, next door to the house where I was born in upper Illinois.

Last summer, in Minneapolis, I was astounded by a vast ocean of dandelions brimming the entire city. No lawn existed that had fewer than a thousand flowers. I was overwhelmed because in California, as soon as we see one flower in the middle of the yard, we run out and stomp it.

Next year I will send my *Dandelion Wine* play to Minneapolis, and I will go there for the re-premier and run out on one of those lawns, surrounded by ten thousand dandelions, and fall to roll like a happy dog.

HOW SOMETHING WICKED CAME (1996)

If Gene Kelly hadn't danced, *Something Wicked This Way Comes* might never have been written. In fact, it is an absolute certainty my carnival would not have come alive to travel and arrive at 3:00 A.M., the soul's midnight.

The details of creation are such that, looking back, one experiences apprehension. Gene Kelly invited me and my wife, Maggie, to a private screening of his all-dance musical *Invitation to the Dance.* If I had refused the invitation, again, this book would have been stillborn. Fortunately, Maggie and I attended the screening and walked home from MGM that night filled with admiration.

On the way I confessed I would almost tear off my right arm to work for Gene Kelly.

"Do it," Maggie said. "Go through your files, look at all those stories you've put away, find something that might fit, do a screen treatment, and send it to Gene."

"Just like that?" I said.

"Just like that," said Maggie.

One episode in Gene Kelly's *Invitation to the Dance* had to do with a carnival/circus, with overtones of *Laugh, Clown, Laugh,* Lon Chaney's tragic 1926 film.

Rifling my file of some thirty published and unpublished stories, I found variations on carnival and circus themes, most of them put away when I was twenty-six years old, one published in a pulp magazine when I was thirty, "The Black Ferris."

The story told of a strange carnival that operated a Ferris wheel that aged people younger or older, depending on which direction the wheel turned, backward or forward. Two boys, discovering the secret of the wheel, are almost destroyed by the carnival owner, who, in turn, trapped on the wheel, is aged around and around, until he dies, an ancient mummy.

Just like that, as Maggie said.

In five weeks I wrote *Dark Carnival*, a seventy-page outline/treatment, and gave it to Gene Kelly.

He called the next day, wild with enthusiasm.

"Do I have your permission to take this to Paris and London and try and find funding for a possible film?" he said.

"You have more than my permission," I said. "Go!"

He went and came back a month later, crestfallen.

"No takers, no money," he said. "I'm sorry."

"Don't be sorry," I said. "I'm honored that you tried."

With the screen treatment dead, a novel came alive. The idea refused to lie dormant. In the next five years, I transformed the film script into a three-hundred-page novel, *Something Wicked This Way Comes*.

The novel, finished, had rough going. It was rejected by Doubleday, who had published six of my books. I was forced to move on and sold the novel to Simon & Schuster, whose editor, Bob Gottlieb, became a moving force in my life.

Even rougher, the book was optioned by a series of studios and producers. I wrote at least three new screenplays for those studios and got caught in a power war at Paramount Studios, where Barry Diller and Michael Eisner disagreed as to whether the script would sink or swim. The wrangling went on just long enough that I picked up my screenplay and canceled the obligation.

At which point Sam Peckinpah appeared, expressing interest.

"How would you film *Something Wicked?*" I asked.

"Rip the pages out of your novel," said Sam, "and *stuff* them in the camera!"

I scanned the chapters of my book, staring, and he was right. The pages were scenes, the paragraphs were *long shots* or *close-ups*. "Sam—" I said.

But he was gone.

I wish he had stayed. I often wonder what kind of film he would have made of my midnight shadow show.

The film of *Something Wicked This Way Comes* was finally finished and previewed in 1983. The preview was a disaster. My director, against my wishes, had thrown out my screenplay and substituted one written by a British writer who understood Evelyn Waugh but misapprehended fantasy.

My daughters, attending the terrible preview, called me the next day saying, "Daddy, what happens next?"

"I'm waiting for the phone to ring," I said.

It rang. The head of the studio asked me to come over. When I walked into his office, he said, "I hope you're not going to say 'I told you so.'"

"There's no time for that," I said. "Rebuild the sets, rehire the actors, I'll write an opening narration and hire a composer for a new score."

The studio spent $5 million in three weeks' shooting, to bring the film back to life. It was released in 1983 to mostly good-to-fine reviews, not a great film, no, but a decently nice one.

The original screenplay and the published novel remain. Thank God for that. No, come to think of it, thank Gene Kelly for that.

LINCOLN'S DOCTOR'S DOG'S BUTTERFLY (UNDATED)

Several years ago producer David Merrick called Stan Freberg, who was working on a musical history of the United States, sat him down, and said, "Take Abe Lincoln out of the war. He doesn't work."

A similar thing occurred yesterday. My story "A Sound of Thunder," published in *Collier's* magazine fifty years ago, concerns a group of time travelers out to hunt dinosaurs.

They are warned not to fall off a path laid to prevent them from inadvertently crushing wildlife, which would change time and history.

One of the hunters, panicked by a tyrannosaurus, falls and kills a butterfly with his heel.

When the time travelers return to the future, they find that when the hunter killed the butterfly, it changed the entire history of insects. Arriving in 2004, they find that a totalitarian government has seized the world. All because of that one butterfly.

This year I've been working with a film company to film the story. The director and the writers have worked on a screenplay for eighteen months.

But just this week the director announced, "Why don't we take the butterfly out of the story?"

I heard this with great shouts of laughter.

God, I thought, here we go again! The story has been published in eighty anthologies, read by millions of students in ten thousand schools. If you shot a film minus the butterfly, there would be pandemonium.

Fortunately, the producers have hired a new director with a new script and a new schedule, and the butterfly has been re-hired. We shoot the film in March.

Now, consider my film *Fahrenheit 451*, directed by François Truffaut in 1966, starring Oskar Werner and Julie Christie, with a brilliant score by Bernard Herrmann, but with some missing elements.

Recently Mel Gibson said, "Let's remake the film and put back all the missing pieces."

So I sold him the rights to *Fahrenheit 451* and wrote one screenplay. They then ordered nine more screenplays in the following years, none of which I ever saw.

Finally an Atlanta bookstore mailed me one of the screenplays that they had somehow snitched, and wrote, "We think that you might want to see this."

After several fearful days I finally opened the screenplay to page 45 just for the hell of it and found a scene where the fire chief, Beatty, visits Montag, the fireman.

When Beatty enters Montag's home, Montag's wife, Mildred, says, "Would you like to have some coffee?"

The fire chief responds, "Do bears shit in the woods?"

There was a long silence on my part.

Then I closed the screenplay.

I never read the rest.

Fortunately, amid my despair, Frank Darabont, the director of *The Shawshank Redemption*, acquired the rights from Mel Gibson and will write and direct the new version of *Fahrenheit 451* next year.

He assures me that he will not hire any bears!

Now, on to my experience with *The Illustrated Man* thirty years ago. When I was sure that Rod Steiger and his wife, Claire Bloom, would star, I sold Warner Bros. the rights.

At no time did Warner Bros. tell me what was going on in preproducing the film.

One day in the summer of 1969, I had business at NBC Studios with Harry Belafonte, with whom I was writing a musical adaptation of "The Wonderful Ice Cream Suit."

Finished with Belafonte, I glanced across the street and said, "Well, there's Warner Brothers. Why don't I go see what's happening."

I arrived at the studio to discover that it was the first day of filming *The Illustrated Man* and no one had bothered to tell me. By accident I had my picture taken with Rod Steiger, laid out on a makeup table, having his body illustrated.

With the film finished, I learned that it had been written by a real estate agent from New Jersey.

A real estate agent from New Jersey!

The screenplay began in the middle of "The Veldt" rather than at the beginning, so that all suspense was gone. Then a dozen four-letter words exploded. The film could not be shown to my young readers, who, by the millions, had read the story in schools.

On the night of the premiere of *The Illustrated Man*, I arrived to see lines of fans around the block waiting to see their favorite book.

My heart sank.

When the film was over, a small boy stared into my face and cried, "Mr. Bradbury, what *happened*?"

Tears welled in my eyes. "My dear child," I said, "you'll never know."

This year I've finished a new script of *The Illustrated Man* to be produced by Columbia TriStar. I'm quite proud of the script I've delivered; it doesn't smell of real estate or New Jersey.

Two weeks ago Columbia TriStar called and said, "We like your script, but we must hire a new writer to come give it a polish."

In my mind I thought, What kind of polish? S—— or Shi-nola!?

I recall my experience at Universal forty-five years ago when I wrote a story called *It Came from Outer Space*. I warned the studio that they shouldn't bring the aliens, the creatures from another world, out into the light.

When the film was previewed, my God, what had they done but bring the aliens fully out into the sunlight—not terrifying but hilarious.

Several years ago 20th Century Fox called me in and asked me to write a screenplay about an Egyptian princess. They gave me a copy of Emil Ludwig's *Cleopatra* and asked my opinion. After looking at this tremendous volume, I realized that for all the supposed knowledge it contained, very little was known about Cleopatra.

I went back to 20th and suggested to them that while I couldn't do the screenplay, I had two authors to recommend to them.

They said, "Who?"

I replied, "Shakespeare and George Bernard Shaw."

The 20th Century Fox producers were shocked; they thought I was joking.

I said, "No, take Shakespeare's *Antony and Cleopatra* and Shaw's *Caesar and Cleopatra* and put them together, and you might have a remarkable film." At which point I left the studio.

Not long after, I was employed at MGM doing a screenplay,

of *The Martian Chronicles*, at which time I predicted that three days after turning in my screenplay, I would be fired.

Along the way they were producing *Mutiny on the Bounty* at the studio. I had a chance to visit the set and watch my friend, Sir Carol Reed, try to make do with Marlon Brando.

Every evening at five o'clock, Sir Carol came to my office, closed the door, fell back against it, eyes closed, and moaned, "Oh, Ray, oh, Ray!" He couldn't possibly tell me the problems he was going through working on *The Bounty* with Brando.

One day I visited the set and saw that everybody looked incredibly happy. I thought, My God, I bet they fired Sir Carol Reed as a result of the trouble with Brando and have got a new director. Sure enough, Lewis Milestone was hired, and within days he and Brando were fighting.

In the midst of all this, the studio came to me and asked me to take over revising and finishing the screenplay of *Mutiny on the Bounty*. Recalling what I had seen on the set and remembering Sir Carol leaning against my door, eyes shut, moaning "Oh, Ray, oh, Ray!" I turned down the offer.

In the years since both films have come out, I've had recurrent nightmares in which Cleopatra's barge sails down Motor Avenue one way and the *Bounty* sails up Motor Avenue the other way to collide in front of my house and sink out of sight, taking the two studios with them.

Well, that's it. Here, then, we have the story of Abraham Lincoln. With Stan Freberg, I hope to get Lincoln put back into the Civil War.

Then next month I'm placing an ad in *Variety* to stash my butterfly properly under heel in *A Sound of Thunder*.

THE WHALE, THE WHIM, AND I (UNDATED)

Who in hell in all the world could possibly write the screenplay of *Moby Dick*?

There is only one answer—

Herman Melville.

And since Melville had come ashore a few score years before my birth and buried himself alive in the customs sheds and was soon buried in the very earth itself, you have an author obstinate to offers. He will not, would not, cannot write the script for the proposed film.

What then?

Hold séances with the miscreant author? Plant the ouija board as funnel above my typewriter? Play Scrabble with his phantom self, hoping that he will nudge you a few words?

None of that.

What's left?

To become Herman Melville. Somehow tailor his clothes to your shape and his flesh to your flesh, and tuck his mind, in one eye and out the other, till it's sewn through your head, again and again.

Which is what I set out to do. It has been the problem, of course, of all the adapters of all novels. But your average novel is a tintype compared with the undersea mountain range of old Herman, where the Great Fish ambles along past the profiles of Roosevelt, Washington, Lincoln, and Jefferson.

In the past the screenwriters who worked for John Barry-more's Ahab simply ran along the shore, ankle-deep, not daring to wade out and risk drowning. The result was, of course, not depth, and two films wrecked in the shallows.

It is all too much.

My God, if you shot all nine hundred pages, you'd wind up with a fourteen-hour film. Great stuff for those weekend family film picnics in China or India. But in America, where Stan Freberg was soon to do his one-minute radio capsule of *Moby Dick* . . . ?

The seventy-minute film dominated the twenties. The 80- and 90-minute films grew through the thirties and forties, to wind up with the 120-minute show of the sixties. How then to dwarf a whale and miniaturize his carcass?

Let's face it, adapting any other writer to the screen, or into any other form, is all but impossible. Unless by sheer genetic accident, you are born with the chromosomes, the brain spheres, the fingerprints of—

Faulkner, Hemingway, Balzac, or name your own writer.

There *are* similarities in writers' natures, and if you as a screenwriter were born leaning into Steinbeck long before he began to write, so much the better. I have always felt I could adapt Steinbeck not because I was *able* to do so but because I *was* Steinbeck. That's a whole different corral of horses. And it doesn't happen every day to every writer.

Melville is something else again. You might as well say you are going to adapt the Andes, script the Himalayas, do a quick run-down on the Antarctic floes, follow a locust scourge south or a swarm of trout in forty streams heading north up some impossible falls. You are never going to thimble-size Katmandu or run the British royal family through your sieve and out your fingers. What, swim across the Atlantic? Cross Russia barefoot in winter?

And yet, impossible as it seems, it must be done. The screen-writer sets out to masquerade for a few months, in the flesh, and look out the eyes of some author.

I did just that. Did I succeed? For a few hours on a particular morning in London in April of 1954, yes. I lived inside Melville's skin. How *well* did I live there? Others must answer.

How did I achieve a moment's visitation?

By reading some parts of Melville two hundred times, other parts ninety times, still other parts thirty or forty times. Some parts only six or seven times; my instinct told me that this or that page, that or this chapter, would not be grist for the whaling mills. Or blubber, if you wish, for the tryworks.

All I remember now is that on the morning of April 7, as far as I can recall it, I awoke in a terrible state of excitement. I imagine it was like those moments we hear about before an earthquake, when perhaps the dogs and cats fight to leave the house or the unseen, unheard tremors shake the floor and beams and you find yourself held ready for something to arrive but you're damned if you know what.

What arrived, of course, was the inventor, owner, and operator, but above all the dreamer, of *Moby Dick*.

On other mornings I had ordered breakfast.

This morning I got out of bed, stared at my typewriter across the room, and marched toward it. On the way I caught a glimpse of my disheveled self.

Now, there is no way for this pink, round face to look insane, lunatic crazy or reasonably mad, if there is reason to madness. What I saw was some sort of purpose, I imagine. A possible raving dedication that would last, if I took advantage, a few hours, never to come again.

I made a declaration to myself in the mirror:

"I," I cried, "am Herman *Melville*!"

And, believing it, I sat down at the typewriter and in the next five to six to seven hours rewrote the last third of the screenplay, plus portions of the middle. I did not eat until long after the lunch hour, when I had a sandwich sent up and which I devoured while typing. I was fearful of answering the telephone, dreading the loss of focus if I did so. I have never typed so long, so hard, so fast, in all the years before that day and all the years since. If I wasn't Herman Melville, I was at least, by God, his ouija board, and he was moving my planchette. Or his literary force, compressed all these months, was spouting out my fingertips as if I had turned on all faucets. I mumbled and muttered and mourned and yelled through the morning, all through noontime, and leaning into my usual nap time. But there was no tiredness, only the fierce and steady and joyful and triumphant banging away at my machine with the pages littering the floor and Ahab crying destruction over the right shoulder and old Herman bawling instruction over the left.

What was happening, of course, looking back, was that at last the metaphors were falling together, meeting up, touching, and then fusing, the tiny ones with the small ones, the smaller with the larger, and the larger with the immense. Episodes separated by scenes and pages were rearranging themselves like a series of Chinese cups, at first collapsed and then expanding to hold more water or in this case, by God, wine from Melville's cellar. In some instances I borrowed paragraphs or entire chapters from back of the book to move front, or scenes from the middle to the half rear, or scenes tending toward midway to be saved for finales to larger scenes.

What nailed it was the nailing of the Spanish gold ounce to the mast. If I hadn't fastened on that for starters, the other metaphors, like pilot fish and minnows and shark followers and sharks, might not have surfaced to swim in the bleached shadow of the Whale. This sounds like fancy talk. Well, let it. Since that day I have advised all writers, on sea or ashore, Capture the big metaphor first; all the rest will rise to follow. Don't bother with the sardines when the leviathan looms. He will suction them in by the billions once he is yours.

Well, the gold coin, small as it seems, is a very largish symbol. It embodies all that the seamen want, along with what Ahab insanely desires above all. He wants the men's souls, and while his soul is dedicated to the destruction of Moby Dick, he is wildly wise to know and use the gold ounce as summons and reward.

Thus, the ship's maul and the pounded nail and the bright sun symbol of power and reward banged to the mast with the promise that gold will pour from Moby Dick's wounds into their outreached cupping hands. Their religious fervor for minted gold runs in the invisible traces of Ahab's equally religious fervor for the true wounds and the true blood of the Beast.

The men do not know it, but the sound they hear of the maul striking the coin's fastening nail is their sea coffin's lid being hammered flat shut.

When Ahab shouts that the first man up who spies the Whale will earn this ounce, a man scrambles to obey.

No sooner fallen than his body is eaten by the sea, which is to say he returns not. The sea is hungry. And the sea is owned by the White Whale. You cannot buy or beggar it.

And no sooner is the man lost in the tides than the tides are becalmed, the sails fall like loose skin on a dying elephant. The ship is fastened to the hot sea like the gold coin forever nailed to the mast.

And in the calm the men begin to fade and die. Exhausted with waiting, with the gold coin on the mast beating on them like a true solar presence, the morale of the men on the ship disintegrates.

And in the long and terrible quiet of many days, Queequeg throws the bones that tell his death and goes to have a coffin built. So in the long silences of heat and waiting, we hear his coffin being sawed and nailed and the whisper as the shavings fall from the proud feather that is the symbol of his tribal power on the shaven lid.

And Queequeg says good-bye to his friend and spells himself into a death trance. How to save him? How to bring him out of his terrible catatonic state?

The book by Melville offers no solution.

One moment Queequeg is frozen and dying by his own secret will, the next he is up and about.

My reasoning went like this: that only one thing could break the spell. Love. That banal thing: friendship. If Ishmael were threatened with death, would not Queequeg from the depths of his own inner hiding places spring forth, summoned by possible murder? It seemed the strong and thus proper solution. Let the men, then, in the first case, threaten dying Queequeg. Ishmael intervenes when he sees a sailor cutting a new tattoo in Queequeg's stolid flesh with a knife. Thus Ishmael proves his love, his friendship. Now, when the sailor turns on Ishmael and would cut his throat, what is more reasonable than to assume that Queequeg, having secretly seen their friendship proven by Ishmael not a minute before, would shake himself free from his self-suiciding trance and thrust between murderer and his bedmate. The answer is a resounding yes.

And in the moment of Queequeg's seizing the sailor to bend

him across his knee and murder him, why then would this not be a perfect time for, at last, oh, my Lord, yes, at last, the arrival of the White Whale!?

Again, yes.

And the whale is sighted and shouted to view. And Moby Dick heaves into sight, as Ahab pounds across the deck and the men gather at the rail to stare at the great white wonder, and Queequeg in this moment of delivery cannot possibly return to his self-nailed coffin, as Ahab cries to the men to row, row, and row again, out of this silence, this stillness, this damned and becalmed sea.

And the men row out, following Moby Dick, and they row into a wind!

Good grief, the lovely wind.

And I had rowed there, all in a single morn.

Starting with the coin on the mast and the wind at last in the high limp sails, and Moby Dick leading them off across and around the world.

What followed, as metaphor, seemed inevitable that day of writing.

Ahab dares to row out of the calm.

So? The typhoon arrives!

And with it the certain destruction of the *Pequod*.

And St. Elmo's fires, which ignite the masts and Ahab's harpoon. "It but lights our way to Moby Dick," cries the captain.

Ahab defies the storm and thrusts his fist down along the harpoon, shouting, "Thus, I put out the fire!"

And the St. Elmo's fires are destroyed, and the storm dies.

And the stage is set for the final lowerings for Moby Dick.

ALL'S WELL THAT ENDS WELL . . . OR, UNHAPPILY EVER AFTER (2003)

It's Oscar Time, so . . .

I have often said, and you have heard me say it, that a bright film with a mediocre ending is a mediocre film.

Conversely, a medium-good film with a terrific ending is a terrific film.

I have, over the years, watched various pictures and, in a frenzy, gone home to write new endings for them or to congratulate ordinary films with brilliant finales.

Let's start with *Fahrenheit 451*, François Truffaut's version of my novel, filmed in 1966, with some excellent casting: Oskar Werner as Montag and Cyril Cusack as the Fire Chief.

But his terrible mistake was casting Julie Christie in two confusing roles and eliminating Clarisse McClellan, the girl next door; Faber, the philosopher, and the Mechanical Hound.

An almost bright film with a brilliant ending.

The finale, with the fine Bernard Herrmann score, shows the Book People moving in a snowfall through the woods, whispering the lines from all the books they have remembered. This ending has never failed to move audiences. The film ends on this high note, and one leaves feeling you've seen more than was really there.

Next, consider *Network*, one of Sidney Lumet's finest films, but with an ending—to me, anyway—that has always seemed incomplete.

It's the story of a network reporter (played by Peter Finch) who announces his imminent suicide. Resultantly, his ratings go up and the network gives him more power, leading to that memorable scene in mid-film where he shouts for people to throw open their windows across the country and yell, "I'm mad as hell and I'm not going to take this anymore!"

When his power diminishes, the network has him shot.

At the finale, he lies dead in the television theater.

I left the film with a dreadful feeling of incompleteness and published my own ending in the *Los Angeles Times:*

If you're going to kill the Finch character, tell the public, so that on his death night his TV ratings go up again.

The next day, hold his funeral on the evening news with Walter Cronkite. His ratings go up again.

On the third day, you stash his body in a Forest Lawn Cemetery cave and roll a large rock in front of it as millions watch.

A week later, you roll the rock aside, find the tomb empty— and you have a television series.

That was my ending I sent to Sidney Lumet with apologies.

Now consider *Rosemary's Baby*, a nice film but with a cowardly *finis*.

Its last scene finds Rosemary, whose child is Lucifer's, searching for her lost baby, kidnapped by a witches' coven in the next apartment.

Breaking in with a butcher knife, Rosemary confronts the coven and stares at a crepe-ribboned crib lying nearby.

The witches urge her, "Rock your child."

She rocks the crib in which her lost baby cries. *The end*.

Not for me it wasn't.

No normal mother would rock the crib. She should seize the baby and race down into the streets, pursued by the witches in rain and lightning.

At the nearest church she should run down the aisle and up onto the altar to lift the baby and plead, "Lord-God—God, take back your son."

Pull the camera away, up in the church ceiling. The film ends.

So *Rosemary's Baby* missed the chance after billions of years to heal the wound between Heaven and Hell, good and evil.

Now let me describe Hecht-Hill-Lancaster forty-five years ago, when they finished *Sweet Smell of Success*.

They asked me—along with Carol Reed, the fine director of *The Third Man*—to sit in on a private screening to help them with the last reel.

It is the story of a man played by Burt Lancaster, a true monster, who runs Manhattan lives with a high hand and with rampant malice.

At the finale, his sister and her boyfriend walk away, leaving him high in his penthouse, isolated and in despair.

When the lights came on, Carol and I turned to Lancaster and producers Harold Hecht and Jim Hill and said, "You can't end the film this way. This man is too monstrous. Learn from the great masters like Lon Chaney that evil must be punished. It's not enough to have his sister abandon him."

I went on: "People come to films drowned in reality, leaving behind heart failures, cancer, failed marriages, bad jobs, mean bosses, and future sickness. What they need is not happy endings, but proper endings.

"The proper ending for this film is for the sister or the boyfriend to shove Lancaster off the roof. We watch him go down and down, to smash on the street.

"A proper ending. Not a happy one, but the one that we all wish for that man who is such a beast."

Hecht-Hill-Lancaster demurred, and I continued, "If you release the film in this form, it will never make a dime because the character, as written and acted, is too terrible. Kill the son of a bitch and then you'll have a successful film."

The rest is history. *Sweet Smell* never regained its cost.

Today, with all the technical facilities available, you could digitalize hands to knock Lancaster off his penthouse. His fall would create an unhappy happy finale. You could re-screen the film and at last make a dime.

Thirty years ago, Sylvester Stallone and director John Avildsen called film critic Pauline Kael and me to MGM Studios to show us their just-finished *Rocky*.

"How does it end?" they asked. "Does Rocky win the fight or lose?"

Pauline Kael and I, almost in unison, responded. "It doesn't matter," we said. "If he wins, he wins—a happy ending. And if he loses, having fought bravely, with his wife rushing to embrace him, you still have a happy ending, because he's behaved incredibly well."

Watch *Rocky* again and see what Stallone and Avildsen decided about the last reel.

Now consider Nicolas Cage's Oscar-nominated film this year, *Adaptation*. A better title would be *Incompletion*.

Adaptation is the story of a cowardly screenwriter and his brighter twin who writes successful screenplays that please the studios. The cowardly twin remains in the shadows, not able to succeed at writing or at life.

At the end, the smart brother dies in the arms of his cowardly twin brother. That is almost the finale of the story as it was played out by Nicolas Cage.

My ending, please, would run like this:

Lying on the road with his smart, wonderful, successful twin, Cage sees that his brother's jacket lies open and his wallet is half revealed. He feels his hand move to take his own wallet from his pocket and shift it into his dead twin's coat. He then takes his brother's wallet so that when the police arrive, he has changed identities.

The cowardly brother now returns to a Hollywood life of success, riches, and perhaps along the way he may learn, given time, not to be a failure.

Which brings us at last to my laying hands on that truly great film, *Lawrence of Arabia*.

As you recall, we see Lawrence being motored out of Arabia by an army sergeant. A man on a motorbike rushes past them and roars down the road toward the horizon.

You're supposed to feel that this is the ghost of a metaphor reminding us that somewhere up ahead Lawrence, in England, will be killed on the road.

Better, I thought, if—with some small license—you have Lawrence instead climb on a motorbike, race down the Arabian road, go off into the distance, duplicating at the film's conclusion what occurs at the start, in England, when you see Lawrence thrown from his bike as he avoids bicyclists on the road.

There you have it. All of my endings.

Oh, yes . . . When I sent my *Network* ending to Sidney Lumet, he wrote back:

"Where were you when we *needed* you?"

REMEMBRANCE OF BOOKS PAST (2004)

Fifty years ago in *The Nation* I explained my love of writing science fiction. Some weeks later, a letter arrived, signed in a spidery hand. "B. Berenson, I Tatti, Settignano, Italia." I thought, This can't be Berenson, the great Renaissance art historian, can it? The letter read: *Dear Mr. Bradbury: This is the first fan letter I've written in 80 years. Your article on why you write your particular fiction is so fresh and different from the usual heavy machinery of literary essays that I had to write you. If you ever touch Italy, please call. Bernard Berenson.*

From this letter grew a friendship in which I gave B.B. a copy of my new novel, *Fahrenheit 451.*

In it, the wilderness Book People memorize all the great books, so they are hidden between their ears.

Berenson was so fascinated that at lunch one day at I Tatti he said, "Why not a sequel to *Fahrenheit 451* in which all the great books are remembered by the Wilderness People and are finally reprinted from memory. What then?

"Wouldn't it be," he continued, "that all would be misremembered, none would come forth in their original garb? Wouldn't they be longer, shorter, taller, fatter, disfigured, or more beautiful?

"Instead of angels in the alcove, might they be gargoyles off the roof?"

I was so fired by Berenson's suggestion that I wrote an outline, thinking, Oh God, if only I had the genius to know some of the really great books of history and rewrite them, pretending to be my future Book People, trying to recall the details of an incredible literature.

I never did this.

But coming upon my note and remembering Berenson fifty years later, I thought, Why not outline Berenson's idea and urge my readers to follow and do the same?

What if you could pick your favorite? Kipling, Dickens, Wilde, Shaw, Poe. These, memorized and reborn thirty years from today, how would they, unwillingly, change?

Would Usher fall but to rise again? Would Gatsby, shot, do twenty laps around his pool? Would *Wuthering Heights'* Cathy, at Heathcliff's shout, run in out of the snow?

War and Peace. With a century of totalitarian dictatorships behind us, wouldn't Tolstoy's concepts, misremembered, be politically rearranged so that various conflicts in Russian society would come to different ends?

Jane Austen's sweet young ladies recalled by a women's libber. Wouldn't they be realigned as chess pieces of nineteenth-century social life as women further up the ladder, full-blown and arrogant?

The Grapes of Wrath might be recalled not as a quietly social statement, but as a full-blown socialist revolt lodged in a dilapidated tin lizzie on Route 66.

Or a semi-demi baroque closet occupant, given the task of echoing *Death in Venice*—mightn't he, thirty years on, imagine the beautiful seaside Tadzio falling into Aschenbach's arms to be toweled dry with laughter in which that Freudian joy might slay the old author?

Or consider a macho dyslexic who dimly discards every third word in Marcel Proust's Parisian landscape to remember his past so ineptly, dwindling to Toulouse-Lautrec size instead of all those languorous perambulations.

And *Moby Dick*. In full recall, mightn't we be tempted to hurl Fedallah, the Parsee, that boring obstruction, into the sea? Which would then allow Ahab to be yanked overboard by the White Whale. At this point it could easily happen that the motion picture, rather than the book, is recalled and Ahab, latched to the White Whale, with his dead hand beckons the crewmen to follow. So the book would be lost and the film remembered.

What a literary parlor game!

List your ten favorite novels, and, in great detail, outline their plots, then renew your acquaintance with these to find out how you have scarred, beautified, or mutilated those incredible books. What a pastime for all of us in the near future.

And of the books lost in the Book People wilderness, which would be easiest to remember? Not the great ones; they are too complex in different ways. But James Bond, easily remembered, could be set free again, shaken but not stirred by time.

Most mysteries would remain intact, and the great poems. Think of Yeats's "Golden Apples of the Sun" or "Dover Beach" or Emily Dickinson's quatrains or the snow poems of Robert Frost. These, in the tradition of the ancient tellers of tales, would cross time to arrive abundantly fresh and new.

Children's books, also. It would be hard to imagine *The Wizard of* Oz or *Alice in Wonderland* disfigured by inept recall.

The great plays, *Hamlet, Lear, Othello*, and *Richard III*, might arrive, somewhat dwarfed, but that incredible language would ring across the centuries.

Mark Twain's Nigger Jim, afloat on that raft down the Mississippi with Huck, might still keep his name in spite of the politically correct critics shouting along the shore. It's a good game. I wish I'd written on it fifty years ago when Berenson first made the suggestion to me.

Go find your bliss, name your favorites, and see if your long umbilical memory has been cut or you are still wonderfully tied to the things you loved in libraries a long time ago.

ABOUT SCIENCE FICTION

PREDICTING THE PAST,
REMEMBERING THE FUTURE (2001)

"Of what is past, or passing, or to come."

That says it all.

The last line of William Butler Yeats's hypnotic poem "Sailing to Byzantium."

It describes the entire history of mankind on Earth.

It tells the whole history of science fiction in a few incredible words.

For history and science fiction are inseparable.

Poppycock?

No, humanity's truth.

For all that human beings have ever thought about is the future.

Hiding in caves, discovering fire, building cities—all of these were science-fictional endeavors. We can see the depiction of possible futures scrawled on cave walls in southern France, where the first science-fiction tales illustrated how to find, kill, and eat the wild beasts.

The problems that faced primitive man had to be solved. They dreamed answers to dire questions; that is the essence of the fiction that becomes science. Once a vivid dream was realized in their heads, they were able to act on it. So the creatures of old time planned for tomorrow and tomorrow and tomorrow. What is true of them certainly is true of us. We wonder about tomorrow morning, tomorrow evening, and the day after that, so as to plan our schools, marriages, and careers. Everything that we do has to be imagined first.

In the castle walls at Pierrefond are embedded cannonballs that signified the destruction of walled cities forever. The land barons who inhabited them had dreamed walls to a certain height and a certain thickness. Their fictional dreams had reared the castles, and now the invention of gunpowder and the cannon was a fiction made real that brought the castles down, to change history.

When Cortés invaded Mexico, for every one of his conquistadors who died, one hundred of Montezuma's men were destroyed because of a dream of destruction, a fictional concept that made a reality of the guns the Spaniards carried.

In the further fictions that became dreams in American history, the invention of the repeating rifle and the Gatling gun did away with the Indian tribes as we moved across the country.

All, all of it fictions that became sciences and technology.

I must have realized this at a very young age when I skimmed through the pages of *Science and Invention*, which was starting to make great leaps into future space. Covers of the old science-fiction magazines were filled with incredible cities that towered skyward.

I looked around at my small town, Waukegan, Illinois, and found something horribly missing.

I began to imagine those impossible cities and draw them in place.

Two amazing things happened in my ninth and tenth years:

Buck Rogers in the 25th Century appeared in American newspapers in October 1929, the start of the Great Depression.

That one strip's concussion shook me into a new life.

In that strip I saw Buck Rogers stagger from a cave, where he had slept for five hundred years in suspended animation, to see

Wilma Deering flash through the sky, firing a rocket pistol. Looking up, Buck Rogers found himself in a new age.

That one comic strip transported me into the future. I began to collect Buck Rogers adventures and never returned from that long journey into tomorrow.

The second collision occurred when I discovered Edgar Rice Burroughs's *John Carter, Warlord of Mars*. His Mars was a fantastic creation, totally impossible but totally acceptable to a lunatic ten-year-old.

John Carter instructed me to stand on my summer-night lawn and look up at the sky, lift my arms out toward the red planet and cry, Mars, take me home! Instantly, as with John Carter, my soul slid from my body, rushed across space, landed on Mars, and I never came back.

From that future, age twelve, I began to write about further futures, because I found the world around me terribly Baptist plain.

Then the Chicago World's Fair, 1933, exploded. I walked, stunned, through that world of fantastic colors and shapes, where the city of the future was actually built. Entranced by the encounter, I refused to go home at night. My parents had to drag me onto the train to ship me north to Waukegan.

Then I discovered the most incredible truth: The people who had built the fair were going to tear it down two years later.

Idiots! I thought. How stupid that you could build a future and then, mindlessly, destroy all those beauties.

I raced to my nickel tablet and began to draw architectural blueprints of possible cities and outrageous buildings in some reborn time.

Simultaneously I wrote sequels to the novels of Edgar Rice Burroughs and soon learned the truth of what Admiral Byrd had said when leaving for the North Pole:

"Jules Verne leads me."

So Jules Verne, with Edgar Rice Burroughs and Buck Rogers, led me on my incredible trip into myself.

This conglomeration was fused when I encountered Mr. Electrico.

Mr. Electrico was a carnival magician who performed on one Labor Day weekend. In his electric chair, he was electrocuted each night and reached with his sword of blue fire to tap kids in the front row. He pressed his sword to my brow, filled me with electric juice, and cried, "Live forever!"

I thought, Boy, that's great! How do you *do* that?

I went to see him the next day to find out how to live forever.

We sat on the beach and talked, and suddenly he said that he had met me a long time ago, that I had lived before. He said that I was his best friend in the First World War and had been wounded and died in his arms in the Ardennes Forest outside Paris in October 1918. And here I was, back in the world, with a new face, a new name, but the soul shining out of my eyes was the soul of his dead friend.

"Welcome back to the world!" Mr. Electrico said.

Why he said this to me, I do not know.

Perhaps he saw something of the strange future in my face. Something I could not see myself.

On the way home from the carnival grounds, I stood by the carousel to watch the horses whirl, and hear "Beautiful Ohio" played on the calliope while tears rained down my face.

I knew that something important had happened that day.

Within weeks I began to write short stories combining Burroughs, Verne, and L. Frank Baum and his wonderful Oz.

I have written every day for the rest of my life after that last day with Mr. Electrico.

In the years following, in high school and beyond, I continued to write my fantasies and gradually worked my way up from the pulp magazines to the *American Mercury* and *Harper's*.

Along the way I married, and Maggie, my wife, was suddenly with child.

We were poor, living in Venice, California, when Norman Corwin, our radio-director friend, suggested that I go to New York so that editors would see my work. I took the Greyhound bus to New York and stayed in the YMCA. All the editors that I met rejected my stories; they wanted novels.

It was finally Walter Bradbury at Doubleday, no relation, who one night said, "What about all those Martian stories you've published in the pulp magazines? Wouldn't they make a sort of ramshackle novel if you tied them together in a tapestry and called them *The Martian Chronicles*? Go back to the YMCA, write me an outline, and if I find it's good enough, I'll advance you seven hundred fifty dollars."

I stayed up all night at the YMCA, created Mars on my portable typewriter, and showed it to him the next day.

He said, "Here's your seven hundred fifty dollars!"

So *The Martian Chronicles* was born.

Mainly, I might add, influenced by *Winesburg, Ohio*. I read that book when I was twenty-four and thought how wonderful if someday I could write something as fine but locate it on Mars. I made an outline for my possible book but forgot it. Now Walter Bradbury was suggesting a tapestry of those stories, and I recalled Sherwood Anderson's influence.

The rest is history. The book was published to few reviews. In the thirties, forties, and fifties, it was rare for a science-fiction or fantasy book to appear. Readers had to wait months or years, subsisting on H. G. Wells and Aldous Huxley's *Brave New World*.

Then, in the fifties and sixties, more and more novels about the future and outer space appeared. Soon a revolution occurred in American education. For the first time in history, students educated teachers.

They came into the classroom with books by Heinlein, Arthur C. Clarke, Isaac Asimov, and occasionally myself, and gave them to the teacher in place of apples.

The teacher glared at these novels and said, Science fiction—what's *that*?

The kids said, Try the first chapter.

The teachers read the first chapter and said, Not bad, then read on and finally began to teach.

Today the novels of these authors and myself are in all the schools and colleges of America.

Much of this was provoked, of course, by our successful Moon landing. When *Apollo 11* printed the lunar soil, it imprinted all our lives.

Gateways opened to wider fields. Since that time the most successful Hollywood films have been science fiction or fantasy.

So I've come a long way from my encounters with Mr. Electrico, L. Frank Baum, Verne, Burroughs, and, before that, Edgar Allan Poe.

People ask me where my science fiction or fantasy will be taking me in the coming years. I believe that the whole outreach of science-fiction writers in the near future must be in a religious relationship with the universe. It was first indicated in that landmark film *Close Encounters of the Third Kind*, when, in the final scenes, we scan the heavens to see the arrival of the mother ship, which is really an entire city from across the universe.

The scene is reminiscent of the encounter between God and Adam on the Sistine Chapel ceiling, when God reaches down to touch and Adam reaches up to touch, and the spark leaps the gap.

So it is that we fantasy writers must look to the universe and give reasons for revisiting the Moon, heading for Mars, and moving out toward the cosmos.

Space travel to me answers the age-old question: What are we doing here? What is life all about? Where are we going?

George Bernard Shaw, many years ago, believed that the human race was headed in a direction that it could not quite comprehend but would nevertheless hurl ourselves headlong into that unplumbed future.

My own belief is that the universe exists as a miracle and that we have been born here to witness and celebrate. We wonder at our purpose for living. Our purpose is to perceive the fantastic. Why have a universe if there is no audience?

We are that audience.

We are here to see and touch, describe and move. Our job, then, is to occupy ourselves with paying back the gift. This must be at the center of the stories, novels, and films that we fantasy writers create tomorrow.

When we first landed on the Moon on that night in July 1969, I was asked to appear on *The David Frost Show*.

I eagerly accepted because I wanted to explain that space travel was about mankind's possible immortality.

David Frost, however, laughed at the whole encounter, and I walked off the show.

At 8:30 P.M., London time, we landed on the Moon. The following dawn Neil Armstrong emerged from the craft to footprint the lunar soil.

Fleeing *The David Frost Show* at midnight, I crossed London to do a Telstar show with Walter Cronkite, who allowed me to speak the truths I felt were inherent in our escape from Earth.

I stayed up, did a dozen shows, cried all night with joy, because it was the most important night in my life, and for *all* the people on Earth.

At around nine in the morning, I walked back across London, totally exhausted but totally happy.

In front of my hotel, I saw a small tabloid newspaper with a headline which read NEIL ARMSTRONG WALKS AT SIX A.M. . . . BRADBURY WALKS AT MIDNIGHT.

MARS: TOO SOON FROM THE CAVE, TOO FAR FROM THE STARS (2000)

QUESTION: You and Mars. How did it all happen?

ANSWER: Imagine if you will a kid of some nine years seated by the wide-open door of a summer night in 1930. Leafing through his collection of Buck Rogers comic strips with Buck and Wilma on the Red Planet, the boy picks up and reads yet another chapter of *The Gods of Mars* by Edgar Rice Burroughs. Maybe not on the floor, but nearby, are some scattered photos of the mysterious world by the Lowell Observatory. Leaving these treasures behind, the boy steps out and moves across the front lawn to gaze up into the Illinois night sky and find that special red fire burning in the dark. After a long moment, the boy slowly raises his arms, then points his hands at that crimson point of light. Now he shuts his eyes, and his lips move silently, and now at last he speaks:

"Mars," he whispers, "oh, Mars, take me home."

And his soul slips out of his body and sails swiftly and silently toward Mars.

And never comes back.

Who was that strange and needful young kid on that summer-night lawn in that empty year 1930?

You with the questions. *Me* with the answers, of course. Ray Bradbury, born August 22, 1920, in Waukegan, Illinois, destined to travel to Mars and never return from that year on.

QUESTION: Why should we care about Mars at all? The argument runs, does it not, that we have enough problems to solve on Earth without rushing off to another world for even bigger problems. Yes?

ANSWER: No. I was forced into considering all this when I worked on an astronomical program for the Smithsonian's planetarium. They objected to my saying the Big Bang, as theory, happened 10 billion years ago. Well, I said, when *did* the Big Bang occur? *Twelve* billion years ago, they replied. *Prove* it, I said. Well, that ruined our creative relationship, for of course they couldn't prove it. Then I got to thinking about the Cosmos, the Universe, and came up with my own ramshackle theory that perhaps the Universe was never created, that it's been here forever and will remain here forever. Impossible, yet here we are, a miracle of impossibility. My notion is just as valid as theirs. Neither can be proven. But the bigger the power of our telescopic vision, the more immense the Universe becomes. There is no far side, there is no circumference. Now, how in hell, I said, can only a tiny Big Bang create a cosmos that is a billion billion light-years in acreage? It couldn't. Therefore our environment has miraculously been here forever. You mustn't think on it, it'll drive you bonkers.

QUESTION: You're dragging your celestial feet. How does all this tie in with Mars as preoccupation?

ANSWER: I go with Bernard Shaw here. He has one of his characters in *Don Juan in Hell* say that he is compelled to become something. He, as a member of the human race, is on his way to a seemingly impossible goal. He does not know what the goal is, but he *must* go, he must seek, he must find, himself. His destiny is in his genes. He can no more ignore this call, this sum-mons, than he can ignore the beating of his heart. So it is with Man's becoming more than he now is. Not Superman, as-suredly, for that name has been contaminated with misuse. But a creature with a superb destiny.

QUESTION: And can you half guess at that destiny?

ANSWER: There is no one reading this exchange who hasn't at one time or another said, What's it all about? If there is no God, as some say, why are we here? Why have we been created, to function in what way? The problem lies partly in our an-thropomorphic vision of God, which diminishes the aspect of Creation. As soon as you say He or Him, you put Creation in a matchbox and file It, Him, He, on a shelf. The Universe is cer-tainly large enough not to be so misfiled. It *thinks*," therefore we are. The Cosmos has need of us. It cannot exist without an audience. Why bother to have a theater if there are no atten-dees? Why put on a show if no one buys tickets? Why give a grandiose concert if no one comes? Ridiculous. We fill the vac-uum with attention. We see, we hear, we touch, we know; therefore the Universe exists. It is the old saying revisited: If a tree falls in a forest and no one is there to see or hear it, does it fall? Yes, no, maybe? The Universe demands our eyes, our ears, our hands to see, hear, touch, and then for our mouths to speak the wonders.

QUESTION: And Mars is a part of this process?

ANSWER: It is the way station on our journey to our greater selves and our possible immortality.

QUESTION: Big words. Do you mind if I scoff?

ANSWER: Scoff! And while you scoff, we will be gone a-journeying.

QUESTION: Give me more reasons for this time of going away, yes?

ANSWER: We are representatives of the Life Force. Our hidden genetics propel us up, upward, and out. We cannot resist the impulse to footprint Mars as we did the Moon. And when we arrive there, what shall we say to the mysterious mothering universe? "*We* are *here*! Behold, we have cast our seed upon a windless wind in a lonely place that we shall make less lonely. Do we rest now?" To which the Cosmic response must be, "No." There can be no rest, but always moving on. For to rest means to stop, and to stop might well mean a fall back into the dust. In the words of Cabal at the end of *Things to Come*, "Which shall it be?" The stars or the grave? It is a million-year journey. Sleepless at dawn, arise and go.

QUESTION: Your summation of our Martian venture might well be what?

ANSWER: The unknown celestial environment cries out to be known. We are the delegates of cognition whose task it is to witness and celebrate. The Cosmos thrives through us. The dead stuffs of planetary time are roused to life because we say it's so. We pitiful worms have dreamed a cocoon of metal, glass, and fire and have come forth as homely moths and then fine papillons to cross space and annul Time. Our conscious mind *wonders* at this. Our secret mind knows. It speaks. We listen and dream ourselves better cocoons.

QUESTION: How can we prepare ourselves for the long voyage home, a home we know not where?

ANSWER: By an act of forgiveness. We must forgive all our wars and dissolutions, all our criminal sins and terrible exploitations. We must cleanse ourselves as best we can and try to take along the sinless good as proper baggage, never forgetting our history of struggle, failure, and struggle again, encouraging the crippled earthworm to become the gossamer flight. We have been given eyes to see what the light-year worlds cannot see of themselves. We have been given hands to touch the miraculous. We have been given hearts to know the incredible. Can we shrink back to bed in our funeral clothes? Mars says we cannot. The interstellar drifts echo and reecho this. We sit up in our coffins to abandon the Earth's mortuary tomb, knowing that we are the *betweens*. Too soon from the cave, too far from the stars. We must ignore the whispers from the cave that say, "Stay." We must listen to the stars that say, "Come."

As the celestial nomads, we have traveled half a million or a million years looking back at the cliffs from which we sprang, looking up at a heaven that seems almost within reach.

We are seemingly trapped in midstride. Free of the protection of the solid rock in which we hid to invent fire, now we stand unprotected in an invisible rain that showers from the universe and will either cleanse us or melt us to nothing.

Jesus in the desert alone with temptation was a single divine presence. We, this year, with the Millennium commencing, are multitudinous lemmings driven by wireless voices to hurl ourselves into Internet seas where tides of mediocrity surge, pretending at wit and will but signifying nothing.

All of which means we must stop being so hypnotized and transported by the various technological aspects of our society. We are being driven by people who say we must constantly be on the Internet and we must participate in e-mail and get hundreds of pieces of e-mail that we really don't need. We must stop paying attention to digital motion pictures that are nothing but explosions of sound and light.

When I lectured to a group of special-effects people a few years ago, I witnessed two hours of their technical expertise before going on to speak. I then said to them, "I love fireworks as much as anyone else in this world. My idea of something great is being in Paris on Bastille night, July 14, each year, by the Eiffel Tower and seeing the explosions of brilliant color and celestial constellations put up by the fireworks people. The problem is, when the wind blows, the fire is swept away, the color is gone from the clouds, the sky is empty. What you people have done and are doing is fireworks, which I love, but there is no content, there is nothing there when the wind blows. To use another metaphor: You cook up a brilliant Chinese dinner, and an hour later we're hungry again."

We've got to put a brain back inside all of our technological fireworks. It's not enough to have e-mail and the Internet and digital recordings and all the things that lure us to behave like lemmings rushing to a distant sea. The brain that we have to put back in the center of our fireworks is the intent of humanity to survive by higher means, which has to do with the planet Mars, to refocus ourselves not on things closer to Earth, fireworks circling the planet, but on the far aspects of the Red Planet itself. If we could do this for only five minutes out of an hour, we could turn away from some of the most wonderful things that are busy summoning our attention at this time.

We have been given the gift of life but have forgotten to say thanks. Perhaps because we are confused about to whom or to what we should give this thanks. We know that we should pay back but can find no recognizable recipient for our gratitude, which leaves us with the unease of guilt; Christmas children who, late on in the Yuletide afternoon, think all the presents have been opened.

All this because we are at the halfway point in our long overland skyborne trek, our search for our promised selves.

We are weary with travel, we are confused by our prejudices, we are terrified by our hatreds and the impulse to destroy or self-destroy.

Say it again:

Too soon from the cave, too far from the stars.

We yearn to step free of the cave, we long to conquer space and deliver ourselves to the Cosmos.

So the next present to be opened on a never-ending Christmas is Mars.

QUESTION: Can this really be so?

ANSWER: As the Arabian philosophers once said, *It is written*.

After a lecture recently, a young man stepped up, holding his baby in his arms. "Mr. Bradbury," he said, "shall I tell you the dream I have for my grandchildren and you?"

"Tell," I said.

"I'm in training to become an astronaut with Mars as prime destination," he said. "Many years from now, when we have our first colony on Mars and I am there with my family in the middle of the night, one night, with Mars a desolation and dead, I'll wake because of a sound and go into my ten-year-old grandson's area of our smallish hut and bend down over the heaped sheets and blankets and quietly pull them aside. Underneath, what do you think I hope to find? My grandson, with a flashlight, reading a book late at night, against orders. Startled, he looks up at me. What are you reading? I say. *The Martian Chronicles,* he says. He turns the flashlight off. Turn it back on, I say. Okay? he says. Okay, I say. He turns the flashlight back on. Slowly I pull the sheet back up over him. I can see the light dimly under the covers. June 2033, I hear him whisper. I turn and walk away, blinded by tears. Is that okay, Mr. Bradbury?"

I cannot speak. I grab and hold the young astronaut, tears in *my* eyes.

At last I say, Okay.

And suddenly I am an ancient Greek myth reborn to live among disbelievers, summoned by one who believed.

Okay, I say again, and look up in my mind to again *see* dead Mars but *hear* the live whispering of that splendid child.

EARTHRISE AND ITS FACES (1999)

What a shame our new generations were born in the wrong year. They missed the great revelations. They arrived when the curtains had already risen on the miraculous, and so could not gasp with love at the newfound land of Earth.

I speak, of course, of that night when billions of TV viewers first glimpsed our blue-white world in Earthrise, a remembrance of old time, a promiser of futures.

It was, to many of us, the great face of Creation thrust near to enchant us to tears.

It was love at first sight.

But then the second sights came. Peering closer at the wondrous blue sphere in space, we said, "Where have I seen *that* face before?"

The answer was: Never.

Until our time, cartographers fumbled their hands over terrains arctic and equatorial and made Braille transcriptions to steer sailors of seas and clouds. The whole of the Earth was a crinkled maze awaiting the rough guess of sea captains, pathfinders, and nomad tillers of soil. From these palsied reckonings, windblown prints sprang, hoping for safe passage but risking death. Airplanes did the first new chartings, jets sharpened the perception, but it was the shuttle that lassoed the globe to tapestry darkrooms with manifested dreams.

At twenty-five thousand miles per hour, those bullets unraveled photo lightning flashes that drowned in chemistries, rose as revelations.

And *there* were the faces.

A few and then ten dozen mysterious looks. Great continental bodies, vast oceans, and then sharp focusings at this old wrinkled world hid under our spacecraft until in camera.

At long last see all of Earth suspended, they said. Then find its grimaces, up close as the plains, hills, and mountains show how they came to scowl or break forth plains calm of sand and dunes that, wind-washed, erased old looks for new.

All of yesterday was film caught to yield remembrances we did not know we knew. With these multitudinous faces, desert calms, granite brows, and vast Grand Canyon mouths for our foundation, we saw a birthing place from which to fire off toward our tomorrows. Space Station Number One: Earth. Space Station Two: the Moon. Three: Mars. Then take off for the whole Universe.

So fire-furnace scan the following pages, reprint these sightings on your retina to be borrowed as memory.

Here in these masks of dead matter once alive with volcanic fires, wild fevers beneath Earth's stone skin, find the convulsions of the multibillion years it took to wrinkle and gape the territory. Here lie the mute genetic histories of flesh yet to swarm, crawl, walk on its raining surface, to live in caves and hide in towns until the Moon called and they went.

These cartographies, then, are a vast and curious stage on which, invisible, we performed our hates, our loves, our sounds and furies signifying *everything*!

The charts lie here, dead. We rise here, alive, to see its mortalities and find ourselves special in a careless universe. Yet *we* care and vow to clean the stage, prepare its steppes, fjords, and ocean ponds for a mankind grateful to *be*, and careful of the way it treads this Earth.

Now gaze at these territorial maps that save old time to provision the new.

To be seen, the charts say, to be known, they add, and to be loved is their final word.

FALLING UPWARD,
OR
WALKING BACKWARD TO THE FUTURE (1999)

Sometimes an idea is of such size that by its very loom and weight, it seizes other ideas swiftly toward it in collision.

The idea here is, How did I arrive in this future that, just a few years ago, was sight unseen?

The scramble of concepts that hit me this morning reminds me of the famed general who leaped onto his horse and rode off in all directions.

Let me align the scramble.

Federico Fellini once said, "Don't tell me what I'm doing, I don't want to know."

I have tried to live that way: Do things, then find out what you've done. Everything *after* the fact, the event.

Then again, my encounters with the Irish forty years ago convinced me that they could leap off cliffs and fall upward. Witness Wilde, Shaw, and Yeats. Taking chances.

Or, in reverse, jump off cliffs as I do and build your wings on the way down. No blueprints, no plans. Just jump.

Or hear the advice of Juan Ramón Jiménez: "When they give you ruled paper, write the other way."

Or finally, when I was twelve, I witnessed two dinosaur species at the Chicago Century of Progress: the Sinclair Oil's frozen-in-place papier-mâché beasts, plus those beautiful-beyond-belief prehistoric monsters alive, alive! that confronted you when you stepped onto a moving platform that slid you into a 10-million-years-ago Past where pterodactyls kited and *Tyrannosaurus rex*es shrieked, the world's first animatronic terrors, enough to fill my day and haunt my prepuberty dreams.

My problem was, the damned moving platform circled you swiftly past the nightmares and out in four minutes! You had to pay another quarter for a prehistoric jaunt. But I *had* no surplus quarters. One ride was *it*!

Panic. Madness. What to do? How to focus the beasts and save the terror?

By walking backward.

Amid the nightmare kites and bloody carnivores, I simply turned—and walked backward! So that—watch! I stayed in *one place*!

Laughing wildly at my crazed inspiration, I lingered on and on, pacing the incredible samurai beasts.

Chortling in triumph, I walked backward for half an hour, as the other travelers were hauled out and dropped in the reality of a Chicago without flavor.

I almost struck up a conversation with these mechanical thunder lizards when my laughter attracted the proprietors of the ride.

Seeing me not as a wild enthusiast but a roadblock on the moving platform, they lurched in and strong-armed me out into the bright fair pavilion as the sounds of my ravenous meat-eating friends faded and were lost.

But I had feasted well. A billion years of mad animal excursions filled in my eyes, ears, and blood.

Walking backward! I thought I must do that often, to see where I came from, where I am, and let the future come as surprise.

Presto! I have run reversed the rest of my days.

By pretending not to think on the future, I have arrived.

For it was obvious that I wanted to live in tomorrow anyway. When my parents dragged me, yelling, out of the fair that night, I protested. My Waukegan home was no place for a boy reborn as *T. rex*. And then of course I had been surrounded all day by rainbow architectures of such beauty they stilled my heart. I wanted to climb those grand pavilions and stay forever. To hell with vanilla-pudding, dreamless small towns.

So I was trucked out of the fair, shoved onto the train, and I saw the future's incredible promises diminish down the track.

Within a week I started drawing blueprints of improbable cities. I did not look up at lifeless Waukegan, but lived inside my inept dream prints.

FADE OUT, FADE IN:

Those dinosaurs delivered me to tomorrow in ways I could not imagine.

Carrying that prehistoric delirium with me through high school, I met a young man my age, Ray Harryhausen, who built dinosaurs in his garage and sparked motion on 16-millimeter film, animating their brute lives and deaths.

It was instant friendship. We promised to grow old, but never grow up, together: I to write screenplays for primal beasts, he to rear their shadows on the silver screen.

Along the way I wrote a story about a dinosaur wakened from the deeps of time, called by a foghorn, and swam for an encounter with an imagined beast to discover it was just a sounding lighthouse and not living flesh, then tore the light-house down and died, broken on the beach.

That story and the memory of walking backward through Chicago's multimillion-year remembrance brought me John Huston. Reading that story made him think I was Herman

Melville's bastard son, so he gave me a job of rendering the White Whale's flesh into screenplay close-ups in *Moby Dick*, with Gregory Peck to run the harpoons.

AGAIN FADE OUT, FADE IN: Nine years later there was a knock at my front door. Opening it, I discovered two gentlemen representing the United States Pavilion being built to open the New York World's Fair in 1964.

"Mr. Bradbury," they said, "we have come to give you a fifty-million-dollar building."

"Come in, come in!" I cried.

With them seated I said, "What's this all *about*?"

"*This*," said one of the gents, and laid an essay on the table, "The Ardent Blasphemers" (see page 170) which I had written as preface to *20,000 Leagues Under the Sea*, noting the resemblances between Captain Ahab and his Whale and mad Captain Nemo and his *Nautilus* submarine.

No one else had noticed, or written about, the fact that Jules Verne had probably read Herman Melville. The evidence lay in the first chapter of *20,000 Leagues*. When the *Nautilus* arrives on scene, it is described as *Moby Dick*!

I had written exactly that in my essay! Mad Nemo. Mad Ahab, light twin and dark. Now here were these gents.

"Reading your introduction," they said, "we feel you're the very writer to deliver us a blueprint for the entire floor of the United States Pavilion. Can you create a four-hundred-year history of America in seventeen minutes flat, with a full symphony orchestra?"

"Yep," I said.

"You're hired," they said.

And the dinosaur boy who walked backward through time one summer day in 1932, who shrieked protests at being lugged home to the real, who screenplayed beasts and sank the Great White Whale, was delivered to the topmost interior of the United States Pavilion, where, gliding on a circular track as big as a football field, he wept in disbelief that by long ago stepping in reverse, he had fallen into Now.

All hail the precipitous domino effect. My U.S. Pavilion, falling athwart the Disney people next door at the fair, caused them to send a similar message.

"We, too, have a fifty-million-dollar building to offer. Can you write a two-thousand-year communication history in *twelve* minutes flat with a full symphony orchestra?"

"Yep," I said, and helped rear that huge golf ball, Spaceship Earth, a geodesic Epcot Center. A journey from cave to Ben Franklin's lightning shocks, to Apollo's Moon and beyond.

When Uncle Walt's clones restructured their rocket/space ride, they asked me to weather their brainstorms.

Why not, I said, fly the rockets clockwise one way and fly the solar system's planets *anti*clock. The two orbits in opposite directions would give the illusion of double speeds.

"?*!" cried Walt's Imagineers.

And retrofitted the Orbitron ride.

Someone's always at the door lugging façades in need of back porches.

So I redesigned downtown L.A. in my sleep.

When the architect Jon Jerde was nabbed to save lost downtown San Diego, he nudged me to write "The Aesthetic of Lostness," in which I claimed the great joy of travel was standing in mid-London, -Paris, or -Rome, wondering where in hell you *were*! Being lost and safe was akin to sex, or its next-door neighbor.

So Jerde tossed up the Horton Plaza puzzles and vistas.

Standing beyond, you could stare and yelp, "Yep. I could get *lost*! Gangway!"

Prostitutes, homeless, drunkies, dopesters bailed out. Tourists swarmed in. San Diego was rescued from time's trash heap.

Century City in west L.A. poured half a billion bucks into their new mall complex, which did a fast freeze. You could fire a cannon down its aisles at noon and bruise no one.

"Put out more flags," I said. "Plant two hundred chairs, tables, and umbrellas with thirty first-class restaurants to surround them. People go out to eat, not shop. Then, full of pasta and white wine, they'll buy tons of things they don't need. While you're at it, throw in twelve cinemas and a bookshop that would drive Thomas Wolfe wild with unread choices."

"Why didn't *we* think of that?" said the Century City planners.

"*Do* it," I said.

They did.

Fire cannonballs down their alleys today and you'd roadkill three thousand people.

You get the idea.

I am Caesar's Praetorian Guard whispering, "You are huddled masses aching to be free. You are hungry. See the bargains. Buy a picture. Get a book. Loiter freely. Sit and stare. Get lost. Have a drink. Be even more lost."

Who says?

The guy who, like the Irish, learned to walk off cliffs and fall up. Or drop down, building wings. Or, given lined book pads, wrote the other way.

The child wonder who said, Don't tell me what I'm doing, I don't want to know.

The nervy brat who walked backward to stay alert to what

was, what is, or what *might* be with that eye in the back of his head.

The smart-ass kid who was frantic for the arrival of the future.

Who yelled at his tourist dad on the road forever:

"Are we *there* yet?!"

BEYOND GIVERNY (1994)

Let's start with a bush filled with more bees than flowers in France and myself bent over to watch and hear the bees burrowing and nuzzling.

Then let me travel you from Monet's Giverny gardens outside Paris, with their floodtides of color, up through the universe to strange suns, alien planets, and even stranger and more alien life and flower forms. Come with me as horticultural astronaut. Bring your 20/20 vision.

Giverny with its bee-loud glades is our springboard seedbed. To visit there year-round is to find other worlds, times past and times future.

It is, in sum, a homegrown exercise in the miraculous.

If St. Francis of Assisi's noon ghost does not manifest there to provoke growth in living plants, speechless but aware, I will turn in my eco T-shirt and trowel.

Given the chance for burial there, I would quickly sign over my dust. For the entire history of leaf, seed, and bright flower experimentation over a billion-year cycle lies there. One could easily choose to lie down with cyclamens, to rise with dragonflies.

Because all of our Earth is Giverny; it's just so vast we never noticed.

And all the unseen worlds beyond our solar system are Giverny squared.

On many California desert nights, I stargaze across what seem to be firefly oceans frozen in a vast lid. It is in those moments that my mind leaps from the butterfly Giverny meadows to the jungle-desert front porches of nameless planets.

Which planet to choose?

For there are 30 billion stars baking on the cosmic menu, minding another hundred billion quite incredible worlds. Choose any one and behold the providence of Creation as you arrive in unmanned gardens of surprise.

Which means the absolutely impossible. Yet it has already *happened*, proving that the universe is nothing if not fecund, a vast honeycomb of furious re-creative activity, dripping with chromosomes and genes.

I once wrote a poem about a light-year astronaut on a far planet, where he stepped forth to a delightful and terrifying confusion of life.

Arriving, what did he behold?
The flesh of Being, multifold,
On every hand, in full purview
The wildest chromosomes he knew
And wilder still the lambent gene
That grew outré and strode the scene,
As if Creation's simplest Try
Grew stuffs and tossed them forth to dry;
And made a tillage of the sea
To summon tides of flesh at tea
And what was left in sea, a race
With half a dolphin's smiling face
And half a liquid water-strider
And half a troll, the rest a spider

Crept up the shoals and there began
To act resemblances of Man.

Peering around, stunned by all this, my space traveler continued:

"That's quite inhuman, cannot be,"
Cried Astronaut, "that thing's not me
Mankind so shaped, hunchbacked, absurd?"
"Ah there," said Allah. "Mum's the word.
Mankind is not a size or shape
Nor tint of lemon, hue of grape.
Or upright pose or opposed thumb,
I beck, and something Special comes.
Creation's need
Is multi-pomegranate seed."
Seed as large as oiler frigates
And saying this and turning spigots,
Time flushed its drains
And made a creature mostly brains, no bod,
So much for looks, said God.

So some future astronaut will far-travel into what could be, if his psychogyroscope is off balance, a leaning into madness.

For he will be surrounded by a million insect nations. Yet not one species will resemble anything on Earth!

Ten thousand breathing semimammalian critters will trudge, run, kill, and be killed on land or in spawning seas where he might wade or dare to swim. Yet not one critter will be like anything ever seen, heard, or touched in the billion-year arrivals and departures of species on Earth. Some life-forms *almost* like. But, finally, outrageously dissimilar.

He will scan, even more spectacular to the horticultural eye, the darning-needle dragonflies of Alpha Centauri's Planet Four as they knit and sew the air above another hundred thousand alien flower species. In battalions of color, growths will explode to bombard his eyes, assail his nostrils, all fresh, all new, never before seen or appreciated by human sensibilities.

And each varietal of plant, flower, seed, and fruit will teach us once again what we have known but noticed sideways, that it has taken from long before dinosaur until long after, for a single flower aching (in our anthropomorphic imaginations) to finally be named. Our wilderness growth flourished for ten thousand generations until at last distinguished and botanically labeled some few generations ago.

Consider, then, if life on this one new planet seems improbable, if not impossible! Imagine, I say, the next world and the next after that. The universe brims and overbrims with ears and eyes and mouths, all locked in misshapen heads, uttering grammars that fit no books and sound so high that good dogs weep.

The purpose for space travel, then, is, roundabout, to see our spines and the fuzz behind our ears.

The imaginative writer Jack Williamson once wrote of a journey in which a man rocketed out to the rim of space only to arise, miniaturized and pollinated, in a ripe sunflower in his own yard. So it is with the super-Givernys we will someday landfall, not realizing we go to learn about Earth better than we ever knew. Giverny, then, is a forecast tasting, a sounding of our travels away from Earth, unto ourselves.

On Earth the locust, in his seventeen-year nap, dreams aboveground propagations to fund more generations of sleepers. So on far worlds, in mineral genetics, life waits to burst forth in fireworks of perception while inhabiting architectures of shell and bone that they will find beautiful even as we witness them grotesque.

The firefly and the star embody our metaphor: Sometimes the stars move, sometimes the firefly holds still; then the reverse. The caterpillar worm in chrysalis imagines wings, then cracks its coffin to rise as new creature, forgetful of the old.

In a story begun but unfinished some years back, I imagined an astronaut fallen amid a terrifying spider race. Panicked, he soon discovered that these creatures with too many legs could spinnet out glorious tapestries that did *not* catch insects but trapped only imaginations. They were beings of high intelligence. In sum, a spider civilization might not *look* it, but was "human." How so?

In my play *Leviathan '99*, Quell, from far Andromeda, explains what "human" should mean:

Too many arms have I, too many fingers, too many eyes, and much too tall and apple-green my skin, yet in the gentlest and most incredible sense, find "human" here. For *what* is that quality? Not to murder, kill, know darkness, not to rape or pillage, not to destroy. Aspirations for all beings ascending toward humanity. Not reached as yet, but the final goal is peace, serenity, and the blood cleansed of violence. Someday, your people of Earth will know and *be* that. My people and myself, thousands of light-years off, dreamed and reached that goal, ten million years before you were born. Neither spider-king nor Earth-peasant am I. Behold my qualities! Am I not—*human*?

In sum, what Quell says is: Judge by actions. Dogs, for instance, are on their way to humanity. They sense the difference between good and bad, know guilt, and suffer sadness. Lacking most of our race tomorrow, would a canine civilization develop to achieve the humane? Or would they still lick our wrists and play dead?

> *So do not judge a spider race*
> *Because it does not have your face.*
> *Behind your eyes may lurk a foe*
> *Much worse than simple lizards know.*

Finally, some twelve or fourteen years ago, I saw the following item in the international news:

Scientists predict, with new gene-chromosome research, we may soon be able to repopulate the world with extinct generations of animals.

Damn fool me, I then wrote this:

> *With recombinant DNA recalled from dust*
> *The Beasts that once were ours to keep in trust,*
> *Shape mammoth fresh and new as on that morn*
> *When all the flesh of ancient Time was born.*
> *Rebuild the pterodactyl, give him flight,*
> *Erect tyrannosaurus at midnight,*
> *Wake brontosaurus drowned in tar-pit deeps,*
> *Go tiptoes where the eohippus sleeps,*
> *And with your recombinant DNAs*
> *Thrive slimes and muds where stegosaurus stays.*
> *Be God. Provoke His medicines. Cry: Light;*
> *And all the lost beasts, waked, raise up from night.*
> *Ecologists, beware! Observe our theses!*
> *You Doomsters now our prime Endangered Species!*

Bright fool he, Michael Crichton then wrote *Jurassic Park*.
I haven't seen his film. I wonder if I ever will.

All this gab, guff, and blather because I happened upon a
bee bush fifty miles outside Paris? Indeed. There were more
hovering critters, humming their joys as they burrowed after
nectar, than there were flowers. Their hungry compatriots had
to wait stacked up for landings. The sounds they made, waiting,
were another blossoming in the garden.

I write this to open your eyes. Or, if they are already open,
to lift them to where the motionless stars write moving histories on the air. Or, if you have stared too long at the sky, to
lower your gaze and find not just Monet's tourist-flocked gardens but the entire Earth beyond: Giverny in excelsis.

ABOUT PEOPLE

MOUSER (UNDATED)

I have imagined but failed so far to sell the Smithsonian on allowing me to fabricate and shock to life a series of garages with shut doors. Open the first set of doors and you find Henry Ford shunted under his first car, busy at repairs. Shut the doors. Move on to the next garage, open wide. Two bicycle repairmen within add wings to their bike and sail it over Kitty Hawk. Other doors open to discover Theodor von Kármán and his Caltech students inventing the Jet Propulsion Lab to take us to Mars, Jupiter, Pluto, and beyond. Yet another door opening, and a young chap named Wozniak is blueprinting and wiring an Apple as big as the world.

Now, quickly, back to Garage Number Three, which we have not as yet opened. Open it.

Inside, a man with a mustache, drawing a mouse.

A mouse that one day would stand astride the world.

Born in a garage in Glendale, California, in 1922.

The man is Walt Disney.

Shall I tell you how first I met him and what happened then?

Yes. But first encounters first. Sometime in 1928 in a dark theater in Waukegan, Illinois, I saw the Disney Studio's wondrous sound film *Steamboat Willie*. That was super, but what happened soon after rooted me, walking backward in the dark.

Skeleton Dance.

It was a five-minute lightning bolt that knocked the soul out of my eight-year-old body and vacuumed it back in, bright, clean, refurbished, hyperventilated, new. I loitered all day in the Genesee Theatre just to see that incredible five minutes of drawn terror and delight reinvent itself on the vast screen. Those skeleton acrobats, catapulting their bones about a grave-yard and bounding out of tombs and shoving their skulls at a special boy in the front row center, caused him to sit through two performances of some dumb Adolphe Menjou let's kiss again and cause a run on disgusted boys bolting back and forth to the men's room and drinking more pop to make more pee. In the middle of this racetrack routine, having seen the skeletons perambulate in syncopation for the third time, my father ap-peared and dragged me babbling home to a cool reception and a cool dinner.

I joined the Mickey Mouse Club not long after, and every Saturday for four or five years saw every Mickey Mouse and Silly Symphony ever made, at least twice each matinee. I had been there when Disney added sound and music to his car-toons. I was there when he painted the cels and added color.

I was there opening day in Los Angeles to see *Snow White and the Seven Dwarfs*, eight times in the first two weeks, paying twice, the remainder sneak-ins.

I was the nineteen-year-old newsboy selling the *Herald* every afternoon for a year in 1940 raising a fist and shouting at God, "If you let a car kill me here in traffic before *Fantasia* opens, you're in *big* trouble!" I lived in terror of being struck dead be-fore I had seen the greatest film in world history. My judgment was right. It was. Give or take some room for *Citizen Kane*.

It's been the long way 'round to my meeting Disney. Thanks for waiting. Here he comes.

At Christmas in 1964, I was wandering through I. Magnin's

vast Beverly Hills store when I saw a man advancing up the aisles with his chin tucked over an armload of gifts.

My God, I thought, my hero!

The Mouse Maker of skeletons and ducks and dragons himself.

I dashed up to him and cried, "Mr. Disney?"

"Yes?" he said.

"My name is Ray Bradbury."

"I know your books," said Walt.

"Thank God," I said.

"Why?" Walt said.

"Because someday soon," I said, "I want to take you to lunch."

There was a long pause while Disney took a breath, smiled, and replied, "Tomorrow?"

Tomorrow. My God, when was the last time you heard someone say that? It's usually next week, next month, next year. Don't call me, I'll call you. But . . .

Tomorrow!

And tomorrow it was, seated at a card table in his studio office, devouring soup and salad and babbling. His was quiet, mine was loud. I lived the hour, tasting nothing, my home-grown skeleton rattling with joy every time Walt asked a question or served an answer.

We talked a dozen things in one hour. I had been warned by Walt's secretary that I must leave promptly at one, as his was a busy schedule. So we ran up and down lists of loves and hates. Above all, we hated people who put up world's fairs one year and ripped them down twenty months later. Why not leave one up forever to recharge batteries young and old, spin people through what I called Schweitzer's centrifuge, which meant Do something wonderful, someone may imitate it. World's fairs, with museums, were the concrete realizations of impossible dreams. Their purpose to so stun you with the past that you spun in circles in the present and charged off to revamp the Future. I had already contributed to such an overflow of ideas and rambunctious creative behavior by writing a four-hundred-year history of the United States, seventeen minutes in length, with narrator and full symphonic orchestra for the United States Pavilion at the New York World's Fair earlier that year. Walt had seen, heard, and liked my prose poetry declaimed by John McIntire, hence this rattling good lunch. Promptly at one I leaped to my feet, seized his hand, and said good-bye. "Hold on," said Walt.

And steered me out for a go-round of visits to the then-building People Mover, a new hippo for the Jungle Ride, and an improved Gettysburg-speaking robot Lincoln. When we wandered back into Walt's office, it was after three, two hours late. His secretary skewered me with her stare. No, I pantomimed, pointing to Walt, him!

How come? Obviously he had X-rayed the skeleton dance in my face, along with Maleficent, more than a hundred Dalmatians, the twilight bark, and a clutch of *Fantasia* dinosaurs lumbering into eternity. He could have read in a dark room by the light in my cheeks. He had to respond to that.

There followed a series of lunches with all the men who had created *Snow White, Bambi,* and Disneyland itself. They all knew how I had written letters to uncounted magazines defending the Magic Kingdom against the cold marble New York intellectuals whom I challenged to sail just once on the Jungle Boat, where I had traveled with Charles Laughton to watch him transmogrify into Captain Bligh on the instant. I had soared with him over Big Ben at midnight and decided if it was good enough for Charles Laughton, one of our greatest actor/directors, it was good enough for me.

I watched the blueprinting and laying of the foundations for the Pirates of the Caribbean and the Haunted Mansion, meanwhile planning and replanning cities and malls in my head. One lunchtime I said that Los Angeles needed a really good creative mayor like Walt. His swift response:

"Why should I be mayor, when I'm already king?"

No argument.

At our almost-final lunch, Walt turned to me and said, "Ray, you've done so much for us, what can we do for you?"

Without hesitation I said, "Open the vaults."

Without hesitation he picked up the phone, dialed a number, and said, "Open the vaults. I'm sending Ray over. Let him take anything he wants."

Open the vaults! My God! Hurrying, not walking, across the studio street to the archives, I recalled my first days in Los Angeles when I was fourteen, going to the L.A. Museum every Sunday at noon to visit one small room where they had laid out, under glass, single animation celluloid panels with images of *Skeleton Dance*, *Steamboat Willie*, and *Flowers and Trees* on display. I devoured these and came back week after week, month after month, for years, loving and desiring to own just one, just one single cel! And here I was on my way to filch and carry, carry and filch, give me some of these, some of those, from the candy store.

In the vaults that lay open, I forgot how to breathe or see, the selection was so vast and historical and life-threatening. I grabbed cels from *Snow White and the Seven Dwarfs*, *Sleeping Beauty*, *Alice in Wonderland*, *Bambi*, *Fantasia*, and not only cels but drawings, sketches, watercolors. I had nothing to carry them in so had the archivist load my arms. Clutching some

twenty or thirty pounds of my most dearly dreamed life, I staggered out through the studio gates, fearful of being arrested by
some art police, lurched into my taxicab, and drove home, looking back, wondering what was wrong with these people that
they didn't realize I was stealing from the Louvre, the Smithsonian, and the Washington, D.C., National Gallery.

Years later every single cel that I clutched in my arms towered in value to ten thousand, twenty thousand, or one hundred thousand dollars apiece. One cel alone, the Dwarfs
washing their hands in a tub, with fully illustrated background,
would have brought two hundred thousand from such as
Steven Spielberg, who destroyed the competitive market in the
late seventies by throwing a walletful of thousand-dollar bills
into the auction.

But then, there, on that day, in that taxi, with me running
like a thief in broad daylight, no one cared. I was the rare idiot
in the museum stillness, age thirteen, who had devoured, digested, and distilled animation cels directly from eyeballs to
heart's blood. I was the crazed enthusiast who spent all the
money I earned, ten bucks a week, to buy tickets to *Fantasia* in
1940, watching my friends' faces in the dark, and if they didn't
like the dinosaurs, ostriches, hippos, and that gesticulant Lucifer atop Bald Mountain, off with the friendship! Forever.

I was the one who, at Disneyland, four or five times a year
from 1956 to 1964, bought cels for five bucks apiece from trays
in Tomorrowland, where they lay neglected by nonappreciative
dumbos. I already had one hundred or more cels picked up in
an almost free market. Now, with incipient heart failure, I was
rocketing home carrying *Mona Lisa*, *Guernica*, and *The Last
Supper*. Hell, no, *better* than that. At home, where the cels still
live today, I waited for an archivist's telephone call to damn

well lug back the stolen goods. It never came. I suffered a meltdown of bliss.

Lunches with Walt grew more infrequent. There were rumors of illness and impending mortality. His death, to me, was a death in the family.

Late in 1966 I got a phone call from Richard Shickel, who was writing Walt's biography. I was supposed to have lunch with Shickel, and on that day he called with the news that Walt was gone. Did I want to cancel lunch? My God, no, I said, there's all the more reason to see you now, so I can tell all I know about the Mouse and the Mouser. At the end of his book, Shickel quoted Walt's remark about not being mayor, preferring to be king.

Rumors began immediately that Walt had been flash-frozen, to be opened in another year for some future life.

Nonsense, I protested. His life had been so full and rich and royal he didn't need to be turned into a 2001 Popsicle.

The lies still persist. So much for royalty.

On the day of Walt's funeral, CBS Radio telephoned to interview me. My wife answered and on the air, live, told CBS I wasn't home.

Where was I?

On my way to Disneyland with my four daughters.

When I returned with the kids late at night and heard of my wife's remarks broadcast on the CBS Network, tears burst from my eyes.

What a grand epitaph for a man who had caught, inspired, and changed my life.

Only for the good.

LORD RUSSELL AND THE PIPSQUEAK (UNDATED)

In the spring of 1954, when the screenplay of *Moby Dick* was almost finished, a letter arrived at my London publishers. Addressed to my editor, Rupert Hart-Davis, it was from Bertrand Russell, the world-famous philosopher whose *History of Western Philosophy* I had read some years before, discovering it to be then, and still now, the finest all-around analysis of the great thinkers of modern times. The letter indicated the pleasure that Lord Russell had taken in my recently published novel *Fahrenheit 451* and added that if it were convenient, Russell would be happy to welcome me for a visit.

There was enclosed a remarkable photograph of the lord in his study, pipe in hand, *Fahrenheit 451* at his elbow.

I was stunned by this message and his photo and in my numb response did not telephone for days. When finally I called through, Lord Russell answered most kindly and heard me out on my problems: I had accomplished Melville two falls out of three but now must hasten south to Sicily to meet my wife and daughters after three months' absence. Would it be possible, on short notice, to train out that evening for a few hours? Amazingly, it would!

So promptly at 7:00 P.M., I left Victoria Station and was hurled forward much too quickly for my rendezvous with the world's greatest living mind. On the way I was struck a tremendous blow: What, my God, would I say to Lord Bertrand Russell? Hello? How's things? What's new? Good Gravy and Great Grief! My soul melted to caterpillar size and refused the gift of wings. And J.C.! *Look!* the train was stopping at my destination! My teeth did not chatter, because I had bitten my tongue. Hailing a taxi, I left my brain somewhere on the road, and as the townscapes flashed by and my intellectual collision with the grand mind loomed, my panics increased to the third power. What to ask him? What cross-references to parade in an attempt to jog elbow to elbow through mutual libraries? If he mentioned Nietzsche or Schopenhauer, would I collapse in ignorant ruins? What if he loved Sartre? I didn't, having tried to scan his *Nausea* that year, only to wind up with feelings befitting the title.

What if he had known Freud? The closest I had come to Analysis was Edgar Guest.

The panics continued as I taxied a last mile to ring the lord's bell and rock from foot to foot on his sill.

He himself opened the door and steered me in by my trembling elbow, though he seemed a foot shorter than myself.

Gathering my breath, I exploded with what became inspiration. As he introduced me to his wife, who was knitting quietly in the parlor, I more shouted than spoke:

"Lord Russell," I said, "I predicted to friends, years ago, that if you ever turned your talent to short fiction, it would be in the fantastic and science-fictional manner of H. G. Wells. How else could a thinker write," I finished, lost for air, "than in a scientifically philosophical mode?!" I fell silent, having used up all my idiocy for the day.

But Bertrand Russell's nod and smile saved me.

"Yes, yes, of course," he laughed. "You were absolutely correct!"

Inspired, I moved swiftly to describe the stories in his two volumes of fiction. Since I was one of the few in the entire United States who had bought his tales, I was now the rare expert and expounded on their qualities.

They were works from the mind of an idea visionary, each idea vividly conceived but moderately executed. His genius was in the essay, grand and minute, not in character portrayal or the delineation of master scenes. Bertrand Russell was, in sum, a bright amateur seeking but rarely finding the dramatic effect, accomplished only in jump-starting brilliant fancies but failing to breathe them into satisfactory lives.

He was much like a holder of a poker-game royal flush, unable to know how to win in the midst of plenty.

I had devoured his stories, then, for his concepts, not his ability. I could not admit this, watching his smile, so I ignored his final effects to focus on his pomegranate seeds. Was I duplicitous? No, simply young and eager to please the master. Whatever my motives, now Lady Russell put aside her philosophical knitting and laid out the ubiquitous tea. I managed to suck the stuff through my teeth with half-hidden distaste, having learned to consume the dreadful brew in the company of Gerald Heard, Christopher Isherwood, and Aldous Huxley.

In any event, having lit Lord Russell's fuse without confessing his failure to write dramas commensurate with his fancies, we now moved to my peculiar talents.

How was it that I was hired to screenplay Melville? More, how could *anyone*, possessed of a modicum of insight, render nine hundred pages of tryworks, St. Elmo's fires, chases, and lowerings into a sardine-can-size script? Was I mad to have attempted this? Or had I driven myself lunatic, later, during its accomplishment? I admitted to both. Lady Russell knitted on and on.

I described the process whereby I had displaced my molecules, my writing genes and chromosomes by the thousands, during half a year. By osmosis old Herman had risen in my blood with wild shouts to vanquish me and enthrone himself at my screenplay's heart. I told Lord Russell of the metaphors I had re-created, to encircle each other, stolen from far islands in Melville's novel to be reestablished as first cousins, brothers and sisters, sharing a center stage where I had stuck them to behave. Lord Russell, impressed by this, to my delight said so, which left us with the question, How could I have swallowed an ambiguity to deliver forth a visual sermon as vast as Father Mapple's?

Naïveté was my answer. I had dared because I hadn't known better. If I had guessed at the start of my chase that I risked lightning slaughter by the livid fist of God, I would have refused the pursuit.

But, because I was a teenage thirty-three, lured by the symphonic passage of the Whale and seeking words to fit the grand cantatas' flow, I had pitched a wild harpoon to fasten that whiteness and jumped after. Naïveté, I finished, pure and simple. Mindless naïveté. A fool protected by his foolishness, winding up wise.

At which point Lady Russell paused from her soundless knitting, fixed me with a steady and unrelenting stare, and said, "Let us not be *too* naïve, shall we?"

And was silent for the rest of my stay.

Blushed with shame, and realizing that in my pretense at modesty I had revealed an overweening ego, I sluiced down another draft of terrible tea and waited for Lord Russell's rescue, which he promptly deployed. Accepting my naïveté for what it was—a blind mask hiding my young needs—he plied me with more queries about the mysteries of film creation. He nodded approvingly when I revealed that my true genius, if that is what it was, was differentiating a metaphor from a dim-bulb cliché twist when they up and bit me. I was covered with tooth marks from Emily Dickinson, Shakespeare, Tarzan, H. G. Wells, and Alexander Pope. Cornered, I swiftly scanned my bite-mark wounds to find quick solutions. I had not only drowned in the great poets' images but had assimilated Mickey Mouse, Popeye, Prince Valiant, and Joe Strong, Boy Magician. I was, unknowingly, my own Illustrated Man, my skin swarmed with pictures from Gustave Doré, Grandville, and Arthur Rackham, all alert and waiting to flow from my retina down my arms to spurt from my fingertips. I was a teeming mass of interchangeable delights, harvested from two dozen arts and kindred sciences. I had devoured circuses to upchuck carnivals. One being Melville's Shakespearean shadow show and its haiku metaphors.

I had flung myself headlong into the book, I said, in total immersion, now listening to the chart flow of creatures gone 'round the world. I had heard a madman's shanties and, finally, the tidal churn of Moby's flukes giving as good as they got from phantom fires, ghost storms, and hurricanes that crucified men against the topsail ropes to bleach their souls.

Give or take a symbol or aside, I laughed.

In the midst of this welter, I played deadman's drift, a loose-limbed soul sponging in every Brit-filled surge day after day until, waterlogged, I staggered ashore to scribble messages on sand until some few remained as images that named themselves screenplay.

Er, give or take a few hot-air exclamations and senatorial outcries. The whole trick, I ended, lamely, ashamed of my lecture but forging on, was to pretend inattention while sinking for the third time.

Did that make any sense?

Russell, buffeted by my fustian, assured me that it did.

Encouraged by the lord, I raved on.

How different were my methods from the heavy Hollywood industrial attacks by Huston seeking to flense the Great Creature by repeated beatings until the beast was not only dead but buried by fruitless intellects.

The memory was all too recent of Huston pacing back and forth across the Royal Hibernian reception lobby late afternoons struggling to "solve" Melville while I ground my teeth and beat my pate in despair, and tried to force-feed problems to knock forth solutions. I had had to teach John how to leave things alone, walk away once your head was crammed with Spirit Spouts, 3:00 A.M. panics, Spanish gold doubloons, and the rolling of Queequeg's bones, allowing room for the secret mind to move its pelvis and for the secret lungs to breathe, or else we prolong our labors to stillbirth nonelectric eels.

Huston was not convinced of this, having beaten the hell out of uncooperative screenplays for most of his life. He had long since forgotten that *The Maltese Falcon* had solved itself, being a novel in screenplay form that could be shot by using Peckinpah's later advice: "rip the pages from the book and stuff them in the camera!" Bloody of teeth and claw had been Huston's rapine behavior when film scripts repelled his advances. My life had always been turning my back on problems, wandering off to feed them without their knowing, and letting the problem beg to be solved. Two more different ways of creation had rarely met in a Hollywood used to boxing and wrestling matches and the loveless love affair that so many screenplays had forever been and still were. The major studios and their mechanics knew how to oil robots but circled in wonder around live births. They could nut and bolt tin lizzies but few fast sports cars. Being a writer with more than three hundred short stories under my belt, I knew that swiftness was all. Race the idea up to two hundred miles an hour, add wheels and, last, windshields, doors, and bumpers.

Hollywood producers, and their directors with them, thought you could win screenplay arguments with battering rams. I had long since discovered (change the metaphor!) I must jump off cliffs with a great substantial dream and build my wings on the way down. Passion, not intellect, won the day. Producers and their half-blind director friends believed that by being what they thought was intellectual, they could sum sums and equate equations. I knew that they were hammering up Tin Woodmen that, sing as they might, would always lack hearts.

Huston refused to try any of this, and in the midst of wandering without a compass, Moby stalled in a windless narrows, and John and I were becalmed and silent in late December 1953.

Unable to solve a major scene in the tideless water, John and I asked Peter Viertel, who was working on a similarly browbeaten puzzle called *The Man Who Would Be King*, to sit with us for three days of fruitless jawboning. Said jawbones, I could not help feeling, on loan from three asses. Finally, after three days of running on intellectual empty, I rebelled. "You guys can stay here and gab!" I cried. "I'm going back to the hotel! At midnight each of us must put a notepad by his pillow. During the night one of us will wake with the intuitive solution to a seemingly unsolvable crisis."

"Gah!" cried Huston and Viertel. "Don't laugh!" I shouted. "Don't doubt! Go do!" To their laughter I stomped away, went to my hotel, put a pad on my bed, poised a pencil, and, sleeping, waited for my hidden well to fill the bucket.

At six the next morning, my phone rang. It was Huston, shouting, it almost seemed, in the next room. Not believing, he had nevertheless placed a pad and pencil on his pillow and had just awakened to a panic of pure revelation!

"Listen!" he shouted. I heard him out and cried, "Yes! You *see*! You son of a bitch, never doubt me again!"

The son of a bitch, sensing the lesson I had instructed his afterburner to teach him, rarely argued with me from then on. John stopped his endless pacing of the hotel carpet and let me go off to conniption-fit catnaps that solved problems forty times faster than a bad weather of brainstorms ever did.

Having learned something about passion, he never mentioned my calling him a son of a bitch.

All this I said to the lord.

Needless to say, the evening passed. Now and then I sent Lord Russell back to his seedbeds to see where he had found his most favored notions, whilst drinking yet another pot of heavily milked and sugared tea, and quite suddenly it was time for taxis and trains and to hand Lord Russell one of his essay books, hoping he would write a rare motto on the flyleaf. In a small, meticulous hand, he simply inscribed, "*To Ray Bradbury, Russell, April 11, 1954.*"

At the door I said good night to the knitting lady, who gave me her "remember, no more naïveté" stare and tended to her yarns as the taxi arrived and Lord Russell, treating me ever more like the tin-headed but fairly nice chap that I had always hoped I was, fetched me down the front steps and waved me off into the night.

On the train rushing back to London, I cursed everything I had dared to say, much as on those nights when, taking some young woman home from a cheap film, I had hesitated at her door and backed off without so much as pressing her hand, crushing her bosom, or kissing her nose, then cursing, damning my gutless will, walking home, alone, always alone, wordless and miserable.

Lord Russell and I never met again. His signature, stark and uncomplimentary, still resides in my library along with his two books of scientific and fantastic tales, which have never been reprinted or remembered. His solemn smile crosses the years, along with the mute regard of Lady Russell admonishing my behavior.

And so we behave from one age to another, from thirty to forty, forty to fifty, in successions like the chambered nautilus sealing a cell to move on to yet another, leaving one arrogance but to encompass its twin, blind to the new fatness about the ears until time allows a glance back to the abandoned cell to see an ego parboiled, babbling in a semblance of intelligence while friends roll their eyeballs and summon drinks.

"Let us not be *too* naïve, shall we!"

I have tried to behave. But even in writing this, suppressing my naïveté is one more act of pride to which Lady Russell is my ghost confessor.

MORE, MUCH MORE, BY CORWIN (1999)

In 1939 I heard a voice hurled round the world a dozen, two dozen times by the unseen miracle of a thing called radio, then only a few years old.

My God, I thought, age nineteen, what was *that?*

I waited anxiously to hear the name of this lord of all invisible space.

Norman Corwin.

A new name for a new space in a new time.

Like most volcanoes, Norman Corwin erupted at sea level and rose to Mount Everest peaks within a few short years.

Even as Shakespeare and Walt Whitman taught us the love of words striking our ears, so did Corwin sound our timpani to occupy our imaginations.

He drove us with ethereal whips to the library, where, lacking funds, we took his notions, fancies, and towering insights on loan.

If you asked what the word "broadcast" means, few listening Americans could have given the answer: to move across immeasurable fields casting seed in all directions. Corwin was that splendid sower of golden seed. His words, broadcast, lifted a harvest of wild response.

With his half-hour *They Fly Through the Air with the Greatest of Ease*, Corwin targeted and shot Mussolini's son, who relished the sight of his bombs exploding like flowers on Ethiopian soil.

He raised from death the vibrant spirit of Thomas Wolfe, whose incantations, uttered by Charles Laughton, broke us to tears, in the midst of a genius score by Bernard Herrmann.

He directed the first broadcast of Earl Robinson's *Ballad for Americans* and *The Lonesome Train*, Lincoln's cortege locomoting across America to bury our hearts.

In a lighter vein, he rhymed *The Plot to Overthrow Christmas* with Will Geer, dramatized *My Client Curly*, about a caterpillar dancing in a matchbox, a program that was later filmed, starring Cary Grant.

And always it was words, words, words, a love of their swiftly vanishing sounds. *Roget's Thesaurus* in his blood, *Webster's Dictionary* in his fingertips, as a linguist he was the linguini of them all!

The Constitution, and our presidents, had no better friend than Corwin. Early on, he directed a one-hour radio drama with a delicatessen of talent from Broadway and Hollywood sounding the Bill of Rights. Sensing that our Constitution is rarely read, he blew the dust off with the help of Orson Welles, James Stewart, Edward G. Robinson, Lionel Barrymore, and President Franklin D. Roosevelt.

Fifty years later he repeated that feat of political loudspeaking by engaging the likes of James Earl Jones, Stan Freberg, Richard Dysart, and even myself, making virtually real the amendments, name one, name all. His glue fixed our ears to radios or cassette players.

Between times he toiled for a year screenplaying the life of Thomas Jefferson. The film was never produced, but one can imagine it as a forthright portrait of a literary and inventive giant, leaving his black mistress to a sexually fixated film future.

Similarly he corralled the ghosts of Aaron Burr, Alexander Hamilton, and Thomas Jefferson in *Together Tonight*, a tapestry of their writings woven to become a flying carpet through time and landing them, reborn, on a lecture podium.

Lincoln and Douglas debated their timeless arguments, recalled by Corwin.

His *Lust for Life*, starring Kirk Douglas as van Gogh and Anthony Quinn as Gauguin did the impossible, proved the relationship between what is seen and what is painted, how to notice and re-create. The sort of metaphor the film *The Snows of Kilimanjaro* failed to prove with Hemingway's African typewriter.

A few days before the 1940 presidential election, Corwin crammed a hundred celebrities into a studio, gave each four seconds. One by one they jumped to the microphone and spoke.

"This is Claudette Colbert. I am voting for Franklin Delano Roosevelt."

"I am Humphrey Bogart. Roosevelt's my man."

"This is Edward G. Robinson. Roosevelt."

"James Cagney. Roosevelt."

Did it work? Sheer political flimflammery? Yes and no. The job of electing Caesars or jerkwater town mayors has always been chicken in the garage, new tin lizzies out front, and vodka in your beer. Thousand of voters that night might not have shifted allegiance, for hearing was almost seeing. Their fingers itched for the voting-booth pad.

There was no similar broadcast before or since.

His radio drama *On a Note of Triumph*, aired on the eve of our European victory in June 1945, was a singular triumph for Corwin. The drama was broadcast over CBS, a light and dark celebration because the war was not yet over—we had yet to bring down Japan. For those who missed the program, as well as those who wanted to hear it again, it was repeated live eight days later. The country was in raw need of great sun and shadow declarations, and this program helped to fill the need.

After these fireworks it is time to admit my timeless friendship with Corwin.

In 1947, when I published my first book of stories, I sent him a copy inscribed, *"If you like these stories half as much as I love your work, I would like to buy you drinks."*

The phone rang three days later. It was Corwin. "You're not buying me drinks," he said, "I'm buying you dinner."

During that first dinner, I described a story, just finished, of a Martian woman who dreams an astronaut lands and flies her back to Earth. Norman, most kind, told me to write more about Mars.

I promptly did so.

And invited Norman down to meet my wife, Maggie, who married me for my money (forty dollars a week in a good week). And, by God, he came!

Norman Corwin, the world's most acclaimed radio writer, brought his fine actor wife, Katie, to share bad wine and fair pizza on a card table in a matchbox parlor with this errant Martian heading for a far shore: up.

Two years later Norman said the most important thing: I must come to New York and let the book editors know I existed. He and Katie would welcome and protect me. Would I do this?

With Maggie pregnant and sixty dollars in the bank, I took the Greyhound bus to New York, a stack of stories on my lap.

Don't you write novels? the editors said. I'm a sprinter, I said. I have one hundred stories, all bright and shiny new.

Norman and Katie, to console me, took me to animated cartoon festivals and sat me in at the taping of one of his magnificent *One World* broadcasts, which knocked my soul out of my body.

Finally, at the last moment, a Doubleday editor, Walter Bradbury (no relation), suggested that I had already written a novel but didn't know it. All those Martian stories, inspired by Norman, wouldn't they make a tapestry called *The Martian Chronicles*? Go back to the YMCA, said my editor, type an outline, and if it's half good, I'll hand you an advance. I stayed up all night in a hot un-air-conditioned Y, wrote the outline, and sold the book. Norman and Katie flew home, happy. I said to hell with the bus and rode west, el cheapo, on a train chair-car, triumphant.

We met again to celebrate with one bottle of red wine, seventy-nine cents—mine—and a red worth nine bucks—Norman's—and more pizza. What a feast!

When John Huston asked me to write the screenplay for *Moby Dick* in August of 1953, the first person I telephoned was Norman Corwin.

My God, I cried, how do I *do* it?

Call you in three days, Norman said. He called. He had reread *Moby Dick* and gave advice.

It was much like that I got from my eight-year-old daughter, Susan, a few years later. One day I found her deep fathoms under, reading Melville.

I circled her gingerly. "Reading Melville?" I said.

"Yep," Susan said.

"How do you like it?" I said cautiously.

"Fine," Susan said, "but I skip a lot."

"So do I," I said.

So said Norman. Do every other chapter, he said. And then go back to make sure nothing's left out. The whaling stuff is fascinating, but you can't cram it all in. Do *Richard III*, then dress it with the White Whale's oil.

I did just that and woke one dawn to stare in a London mirror crying, "I am Herman Melville!" In the next eight hours, I furnaced my typewriter to finish the last forty pages of Melville's tempest.

Back home the first one I showed the script to: Corwin.

"You've done superb work," he said.

"No, *you*," I said.

Not male bonding, but mind bonding.

Norman showed the way, I could but follow.

It has been said that the voice of history and creative drama, delivered and broadcast, might light-year travel beyond Saturn, Uranus, and Pluto and ricochet on to eternity, where, if we speed fast enough, we might catch Roosevelt's bravado, Hitler's lunacies, and Corwin's rhymed and unrhymed philosophies. We would like to believe that his tripled and quadrupled voices linger in Andromeda because he revitalized dictionaries and recast more words in new echo chambers. He dined on Marcus Aurelius, Daniel Webster, and Homer, blind with bright sound waves for a tongue.

After the silence of ages, Corwin spoke, and the field beasts froze in the fields and listened.

And we were the beasts.

BECAUSE OF THE WONDERFUL
THINGS HE DOES (1999)

No, not the Wonderful Wizard of Oz.

But the wonderful wizard who *birthed* the Wizard.

L. Frank Baum, who has filled our century from one end to the other with naïve joys and unthinking delights.

And what, you ask, are the reasons why.

The Wizard of Oz will never die?

Let me set you a task and make you a test.

Place two books on a table, *Alice in Wonderland* and *The Wonderful Wizard of Oz*.

Then blindfold any friend, steer him (or her) across the library and ask him, with some hesitation, to drift his hand down to touch *one* of these books.

How will the blind choose?

Is there a temperature there, an ambience that sifts upward to one's as-yet-unselective fingers?

There is. And how to describe it?

From Wonderland: a winter landscape, where as the characters speak, you see their breath.

From Oz: a bakery air, the land of the midnight sun, where the day never stops, where noons persist or, if they darken briefly, reburst themselves with pure delight.

From Alice's friends, the contemptuous sneer.

From Dorothy's, laughter or, at least, a smile.

The Red Queen's "Off with their heads"?

Or Ozma's merest sweet-tempered word?

Alice's oysters eaten, every one?

Or the Oz quadlings, in a later book, who, when they hurl their heads as projectiles, still get them back with promises of no more headlong cannonades?

Tweedledum and Tweedledee to help you get lost at the fork in the road?

Or the Shaggyman, in still another book, with his love magnet luring you to innocent passions?

The hand hovers and descends.

Choosing Alice, are you then a cynic, a skeptic, or just a disillusioned dropout?

Choosing Dorothy, are you the impossible optimist, the happy warrior, the convivial far traveler who runs his own lost and found to be always found?

Choose.

I don't claim that we can judge readers by such choices. There must be travelers, like myself, who can go a-journeying through both countries, dark and light, and come forth intrigued, insightful, and happy. Wonderland may be fog and drizzle, but Alice stands as a beacon in its midst, stays sane, comments, and survives.

One might almost recommend a dose of Alice's fog midday, a jolt of Emerald sun at midnight.

Indeed, some of us can traverse both lands with equal enjoyment.

After all, you suffer a culture shock when you shift climates and characters. Addressing a snide caterpillar is not quite the same as oiling a reconstructed Tin Woodman, who remains happy though once he was flesh and blood whose limbs were chopped off for tin replacements. Imagine such a Tin Man lamenting his fate rather than running Dorothy, happily, on the Yellow Brick Road.

Or imagine the Scarecrow fallen out of his field to confront not Dorothy but Alice. How long before the Looking Glass crows ripped his muslin, seeking corn?

To freeze or to bask, these are the alternatives offered by these forever contradictory books. And it is our business here to bask in the light of the road adventures of that eternal boy-child, L. Frank Baum, who could have hot-footed that Deadly Desert that encircled Oz and survived intact, flesh and soul, innocently pronouncing the trip a lark.

Yet another way to look at it is your choice of houses to live in. If you unlocked the door of a desolate mansion minus central heating, a proper hot-water bath, and a kitchen, all knives and no spoons, you must certainly find Alice's Janus friends, two-faced but mostly facing north, pleased by blizzards and bloodless tantrums. Your slumbers would be one long glide off a glacier into a lake of cold soup.

That old baseball rhyme might serve as finale. There is no joy in Mudville, mighty Casey has struck out. Even a slight win might raise the temperature but five degrees.

Conversely if you moved into the Emerald City, best take along fans, sunburn lotion, and a wolf pack to circle your basking hounds, for if you bask too long, someone crying wolf might cry the truth. Summer people are grand fodder for winter sneaks.

Best, then, for the intelligent reader to engage in self-contested tennis, striking the ball and leaping to catch one flight in shadow, one in the lie that says it's noon. For both sides fudge the truth to estimate the climate of mankind at unequal times.

Neither can be proven, both must be experienced, despite the imbalance.

It seems only correct that many of the Oz books were written in a make-believe country where nothing was or ever will be real: Hollywood. Oz could well have been born on the back lot at Universal Studios or indoors on Lon Chaney's Opera Phantom stage. For the back lot is façade lacking back porch and roof, while the Phantom's theater is haunted by flickering ghosts of ideas that bombard our sight without drawing blood. Even murder, in Hollywood, is a falsehood told in full trump, signifying nothing. Lewis Carroll's cast of characters would have died here of saccharine or run back to hide behind the cold glass. Baum settled in, delighted with bright nothings.

And as for the illustrations? I began with W. W. Denslow in my Aunt Neva's Oz collection, as a child of three. I moved on, with equal love to Jno. R. Neill. And now find much room for Michael McCurdy.

Baum, in forever's day, handed multitudinous metaphors to artists who knew how to shut their eyes and see clearly. No match, of course, to *Moby Dick*, whose Melvillean Richard IIIs, Lears, and Hamlets seized lightnings and sank in ten dozen different illustrated White Whale editions.

But Baum with less, does well. This is not the last readaptation of his metaphors by a cadre of illustrators. McCurdy is not Denslow, nor is he Jno. R. Neill, but he is indeed McCurdy. More than sufficient for this new repaving of a road well taken and a harvest of characters well met.

McCurdy is the most recent, but more will follow in the twenty-first century. If the Wicked Witch is truly dead, it is because L. Frank Baum landed on her with his *Boys' Life* Forever Sunkist philosophy. No witch could survive Baum, even today when witches beam themselves up. Cynics and skeptics scatter at his happy cry on what might have been a doomsday afternoon.

Alice and her misfits will survive beyond the millennium, oh, yes, but should Alice ever melt out through the cold glass or escape the Rabbit Hole, she will surely head for the forever-August Emerald City.

So there you have it. Two books, two countries. Two roads taken or refused. Chill your eyebrows, warm your cockles, or stand between, a Twilight Zone of one and much room in your head and heart for both. Down the Rabbit Hole into the Deadly Desert. Over the rainbow to drop your house on the Red Queen? What a fascinating, lovely mix.

Yours to start one journey now.

Tomorrow go stare in Alice's polar Looking Glass, to see if anything human stares back.

A MILESTONE AT MILESTONE'S:
BONDERCHUK REMEMBERED (UNDATED)

During that two-week period more than twenty years ago, when the Russian director Sergei Bonderchuk's quite amazing *War and Peace* was being previewed in Hollywood, and shown, especially at my Film Society, in its twelve-hour length, Bonderchuk arrived to be wined and dined by all the celebrity directors. I was invited up to Lewis Milestone's house for a private reception for Bonderchuk one night. I don't recall if there were any other screenwriters there; I remember only the incredible roster of directors who stood in a line waiting to receive Bonderchuk.

John Ford was there, as well as Billy Wilder, King Vidor, Sam Peckinpah, William Wyler, Frank Capra, Rouben Mamoulian, George Cukor, Sidney Lumet, and on and on, another dozen, all famous.

Bonderchuk arrived and moved along the line exclaiming quietly to each name as he was introduced. With him were two other Soviet directors, whose names escape me.

Needless to say, I was not in the receiving line with the godlike directors. I loitered near the wine and hard liquor. I watched Bonderchuk with awe and admiration as he moved among all the famous and powerful. I was struck not only by him but at being in the same room with heroes from my childhood.

The procession moved quietly, with agreeable compliments offered, but with no great outcries.

Until at last, with all the cordial comments and fine compliments finished, Bonderchuk and his cohorts arrived at the finale. And there I stood, hearing my name pronounced by Lewis Milestone.

The sun exploded. Three Russian faces took fire. Bonderchuk's eyebrows flew up, his eyes widened, his mouth gaped, as did the eyebrows, eyes, and mouths of his friends.

"Bradbury!" he cried.

"Bradbury!" they *all* cried.

Three sets of arms grappled me. Bonderchuk seized me first with an immense bear hug, as he rained kisses on my cheeks.

"Bradbury!" he cried, turning to the twenty stunned directors. "Do you know who this *is*? Do you realize what is this *talent*? Your greatest genius, your greatest writer. My God. Get out of the way! Come! Where's the vodka!"

One of the others produced a bottle and held it high.

"Where are the glasses?"

Milestone brought four glasses.

"This way. Down. Sit. Open. Pour."

And before the astonished crowd, Bonderchuk sloshed my glass full, filled the other glasses to be lifted in a toast.

"Bradbury!" they shouted.

And then, "The bottle's empty! Another!"

Another was brought. They drank me, literally, under the table. There must've been a third bottle. I lost count. I never laughed so much in my life. I never cried so much with joy. My shoulders were bruised from being slapped. My ribs ached from being hugged. My cheeks were blushed with interminable kisses.

I haven't the faintest idea of how I got home. Someone must have poured me into a taxi. I don't recall how long the evening lasted. I only remember being surrounded by Russians who kept pawing and hugging and kissing me, while the two dozen Hollywood directors, riven by lightning, watched ruefully and finally retired to their own drinks.

I awoke the next morning thinking, It didn't happen. It *can't* have happened. I am ruined. All those directors will never call, never speak to me, never hire me. My God, what have I done to myself? What has *Bonderchuk* done to me!?

Well, some of the directors eventually did call. Peckinpah, for one, and Robert Mulligan, and Tony Richardson, and Sidney Lumet, about various projects. And eventually some of my other ideas got made into films, mainly for TV by directors who hadn't stood under the storm of Bonderchuk's inattention and found themselves rained out.

I have never written about that evening until now. Even as I write, it seems an inordinately fantastic time. The Russians cannot have loved me all *that* much. But they *did*. I must be lying through my teeth. I am *not*.

FREE PASS AT HEAVEN'S GATE (1999)

There is, I recall, an Egyptian myth about passing muster, getting through, being allowed entrance, at Heaven's Gate.

Arriving there at some far future date, you will be asked just one question by the God of the Dead.

Did you have Enthusiasm?

If the answer is "Yes!" you're *in*!

If "No"—a hole opens underfoot and you go to hell.

Which brings us to Jon Jerde.

Enthusiasm?

His answer would blow the ears off that dread Egyptian god.

Another Egyptian metaphor applies here. The pharaohs, buried with bread and onions for the trip, were accompanied by pedestrian slaves or boatmen. If their children died, toys were stashed in their tombs so the gods would come play.

Jerde, in his fevers, puts toys, immense toys, not in our tombs but out front, in back, topside and bottom, of our lives. So *we* can come play.

Most architects ignore or bore us with their conceptual ennuis, gum our eyes shut with banalities.

Jerde jars us awake and alert, with his lively sense of fun and beauty, a fused mixture that keeps us off balance. One glance at his outsize toys makes us *want to go in*!

Jon Jerde arrived in my life almost twenty years ago. We

were introduced by John DeCuir Jr., a superb designer for motion-picture sets.

At lunch Jerde said, "Have you seen my Glendale Galleria? What do you think of it?"

"It's great."

"It's yours!" said Jerde. "I followed the blueprint you sketched in the *L.A. Times* two years ago, designing a mall with all its proper human components."

"Am I allowed to repeat that?" I said.

"Why?" said Jerde.

"Because," I said, "I want to be able to claim you as my bastard son."

And thus began one of the happiest years of my life. Jon invited me and DeCuir Jr. to join him one or two days a week at seven in the morning, an ungodly hour for me but a wild and fascinating hour for all of us. We tossed conversational confetti in the air and ran under to see how much each of us caught. We blueprinted cities, malls, and museums by the triple dozen, threw them on the floor, stepped on them, and birthed more, with all three of us gabbing at once. I felt honored to be allowed in as an amateur Palladio with my meager experience but futurist hopes.

Many years ago François Truffaut, that fine French film director, came to visit. What, I said to my wife, do we do to enchant this director fresh from the most beautiful city in the world?

Maggie and I took Truffaut high up on the Hollywood Hills where you could see *our* City of Light. Almost five hundred square miles of metropolitan illumination, a vast seascape of electricity. Then, before he could regain his breath, we raced him downhill to the confectionary confines of the Piggly Wiggly Continental, the most sublime outcrop of the American genus Supermarket. This was 1960, and the supermarket had not as yet invaded France. The Piggly Wiggly Continental, like its name, was a wild meld of sophisticated wines and spirits, Jolly Green Giant vegetables, and items from a reinvented five-and-dime store. Truffaut ran amok in the shopping jungle.

All this a preliminary to Jon Jerde and Medici and Botticelli remembrances.

During a period of employment at Disney's Imagineering studio, I invited Jon out to prowl this rest home for hidden Renaissance sand artists. Except they were not resting but thriving. Anything you might want, saved up from lost time, could be found and summoned back to life here by the sons of the sons of the sons of da Vinci, Bellini, and Michelangelo.

If Jon Jerde's hair did not stand on end, it bristled; if cold chills did not ripple his neck, I imagined them. He became Truffaut at the Piggly Wiggly, a dog glad to see its master after being long away. He moved faster than I could keep up in this sublime territory. Time does not have to die, it all said. Fashions do not have to go out of fashion. Palladio only *seems* dead; sound his alarm clock. Goya and Klee gone? Still *here*! Sir John Soane's Museum in London, with it Piranesis and Hogarths alive, alive oh? Turn left, then right, in Imagineering.

At the end of the tour, I was exhausted, but Jon was fevering his second wind. He was almost prepared to join up with the Mouse.

It never happened. Which is just as well. His brush with Imagineering made me recall a lunch with Disney when he was reconceptualizing Tomorrowland. I suggested he hire me to help rebuild.

"It's no use, Ray," Walt said. "You're a genius, I'm a genius. We'd kill each other the first week."

So it was just as well Jon took other roads with no names and numbers and traveled light.

I was delighted to travel with him for a few hours each week so many years ago. I recall two incidents, one bad, one good, to illustrate how Jerde works.

I sat in with Jon when the Baltimore Power Plant people asked him to reconceive their waterfront property. With John DeCuir Jr., we came up with some wild Jules Verne, H. G. Wells, twenty-first-cum-nineteenth-century concepts. At a board meeting with the Baltimore and some Six Flags people, we felt our bright flags being torn, our Montgolfier balloons pricked, and our submarines run aground. We needed $50 million to start. The power-plant people birthed a midget $25 million, hardly enough to turn on the lights. It was time to leave. Jon gave the nod to DeCuir and myself, and we were gone. The power plant, rejuvenated on the cheap, opened a few years later and collapsed.

The obvious point is, Jerde does not hitchhike any notion that comes down the pike. He is running not to the bank but to the drawing board.

A happier instance was Jerde's being asked to bring downtown San Diego back from the dead. Jon asked me to write a blueprint essay from which to take off. I wrote "The Aesthetic of Lostness." One of the great joys of travel, I said, was being lost in a great city and loving it. If Jon could build his plaza on the principle of being lost and safe and filled with joy, that would be splendid. Jon did just that. Standing outside Horton Plaza looking in, you say, "Yeah. Gangway! I want to be lost!" My input: 1 percent. Jon and his team's input: 99 percent. Perfection.

To sum up, Albert Schweitzer, that good African medic, once said, Do something wonderful, someone may imitate it. Jerde is his good acolyte, his student.

What he has created, let no cynic put asunder. His colony of ideas has caused some few superdoubters who disgruntle his beauties, hate his cleanliness, and resent his changing old times for new. Do not be an architectural Cézanne, they cry, with your fruit bowl rearranging the garbage. There's nothing wrong with tossed cigarette butts, used Kleenex, and fish-wrapped gutter tabloids.

But Jerde's response is that he never met an abandoned downtown slum he didn't love. Love to redo, of course. Get it to take nourishment, sit up, stand, walk, and then win the Olympics.

Some mornings I wake at that ungodly seven o'clock hour and wish I were running with him still.

GBS: REFURBISHING THE TIN WOODMAN:
SCIENCE FICTION WITH A HEART,
A BRAIN, AND THE NERVE! (1997)

In the spring of 1954, when I had just finished writing the screenplay of *Moby Dick* for John Huston, my London publisher received a letter from Lord Bertrand Russell, commenting favorably on my latest novel, *Fahrenheit 451*.

Lord Russell was inclined to let me visit for a short time some evening soon. I leaped at the chance (see "Lord Russell and the Pipsqueak," page 78).

On the train traveling to meet him, I panicked.

My God, I thought, what do I say to the greatest living philosopher of our time? I, a Lilliputian running about in his shadow?

At the last moment, a fragment of opening conversation inspired me. Ringing the doorbell, I was admitted by a most friendly Lord Russell and seated for tea with Lady Russell.

With great trepidation I blurted out, "Lord Russell, some years ago I predicted to my friends that if you ever wrote short stories, they would inevitably be science fiction. When your first book of stories appeared last year, that's *exactly* what they were!"

"Indeed," Lord Russell smiled. "In these times there is nothing *else* to write about."

And we were off on a conversational gallop.

The same would apply today. I dare to imagine that if

Bernard Shaw were alive and aiming his beard, he would fire off rounds of science fiction.

For isn't it obvious at last:

Those who do not live in the future will be trapped and die in the past?

Just as those who do not recall history are doomed to relive it, the above truth is a truth redoubled. For consider, what topic do we talk about every hour of every minute of every day?

The future.

There is nothing else to discuss!

What will you be doing an hour from now?

That's the future.

What about tomorrow morning?

That's the future.

Next week, next month?

The future.

Next year, twenty years from now?

The same.

We are always blueprinting our immediate minutes, our seasons, and our years of ripeness and decay.

How is it, then, that quasi intellectuals, intellectuals, and other haute philosophers find science fiction contemptible? Or if they think of it at all, *ignore* it?

Much of science fiction, of course, has collapsed in a tangle of robot legs.

Too many imaginative writers have not seen the human forest for the mechanical talking trees. They have busied themselves computerizing rockets and rarely questioned any ramshackle philosophy of what in hell to do with them.

Rereading *Back to Methuselah* and its copious notes, I wish that Shaw had survived a few more years to see a remarkable musical film, the finest of all time, *Singin' in the Rain*. Would the Old Man have held still in the cinema dark to watch some flimsy excuse for a technologically creative life? I dare to think so. The film, by its title, might seem to portray a dancing optimist, with or without umbrella, doused but unaware because he is in love with life. But that is hardly the philosophical point of the musical.

Philosophical point?

Indeed. For the film dreams up a future dead-on in the midtwenties when the silent flicker would suddenly clear its throat and croak a song. Not only that but sit up and *speak*. It is, in sum, a fiction about science becoming technology and technology implanting a voice box in the throats of the black-and-white mannequins on-screen.

Singin' in the Rain is, that I know of, the only science-fiction musical film ever made. Delete the music and you still have plot: the invention of sound and its shattering consequence, or how do you construct a philosophy, simple, skeletal, workable, to bridge the gap between silence, unemployment, then reemployment with vocals?

This problem occurs, does it not, every time a new invention looms and threatens? The computer was supposed to throw millions out of work, right? Wrong. It has quickly reemployed those jobless in brighter offices, higher towers, better homes. Television would fire countless radio thousands, yes? No. It rehired them back to run a thousand TV stations as against a few hundred radio outlets.

All of this would have been grist for Shaw's brain, intellectual gum for him to chew in the matinee twilight.

I daresay you could have flashed the first half hour of *Singin' in the Rain* on-screen, shut it off, and then turned to Shaw and said, "What happens *next*? What will sound do to the actors, the studios, the world?"

"Dear Lord! Stand aside!" Shaw would have cried. "No, don't show me the rest. I'll finish the scenes, the dialogue, the whole glorious gallivant in the lobby. Where's my pen?"

Knowing Shaw, a few hours later he would have predicted, blueprinted, and instructed the flesh, blood, and actions of Gene Kelly and chorus, in continuing rains.

Later, seated back in the movie loges, screenplay freshly done under his curiously twitching fingers, as the rest of *Rain* poured down, he would have hooted with delight. "See? I *knew* it. That, that, and *that*! *All* of it! Bravo for Androcles and the MGM lion. Bravo for me!"

I would then hand over one of Yeats's finest poems, "Sailing to Byzantium."

In the last lines of that poem, I found the answer to life, world history, science and invention, science fiction, and Shaw.

A pretty big serving. Let's digest it. One bite at a time.

First the quote:

"Of what is past, or passing, or to come."

The entire history of beast man, man beast, and man from the cold cave to the hot Egyptian sands to the even colder shores of the Moon, and all that lies between. Some banquet, eh? But Shaw would sit down to it gladly. Why? Because the entirety of our past, everything to do with mankind, has been science fiction.

Not much science, of course, and one helluva lot of fiction. But nevertheless, the art of imagining this afternoon, this midnight, tomorrow at dawn.

Impossible? Incredible? Come view another author.

H. G. Wells's stirring film *Things to Come* ran a lot of young men like myself out of the theater in a state of Becoming. In the years since, *I* have become *me*. I was sixteen at the time and needed someone to stir my blood. Wells did just that by sensing in the human animal the Becoming Factor, that need that other animals do not sense. They exist unknowing, but we inherit that extra gene: We *know* that we know. And in that knowledge, both terrifying and exalting, we panic to evolve, do fast foot-work before the fangs seize, the blood runs, and we no longer exist. In that fusion we are less Darwin's and more Lamarck's. It was Lamarck, after all, who said that the giraffe dreams for a longer neck, thus influencing his genes to *become* the long-necked beast stretched up after the high fruits, flowers, or leaves. Darwinians disagreed. It was the fit who survived by their fitness, not through dreaming long necks to align genetics and create a proper spinal cord.

Nevertheless it is tempting to theorize that since we humans are cognizant of our cognizance, we have begun to teach our genes and chromosomes behavior. We dream a long neck, build it, and reach up to the Moon, then Mars, then the Universe. Carl Sagan protests that this is merely survival of the fittest carried to the nth degree. We are the end product of failure upon failure surrounding a final product, surviving man. His dreams and accomplishments are not Lamarckian, no matter how much it seems they resemble technological giraffes with extensible necks that reach from Canaveral to Copernicus Crater. Echoing both views, I have on occasion put together a gaggle of bright companions and entrained them for Land's End or the Cosmos. Riding along with his portmanteau brain packed with notions, fancies, and concepts, Shaw would be in-troduced to Nikos Kazantzakis.

For it was Kazantzakis not long after Shaw who published his amazing *The Saviors of God*. His shout, similar to Shaw's

Life-Force perorations, was head-on: "God cries out to be saved. We are his Saviors."

In other words, why grow a forest and chop a tree if there are no witnesses to the simply miraculous? The old cliché: If a tree falls unseen, *does* it fall, *does* it exist? The Universe, the Cosmos, the light-year immensities existed without eyes for as many billion light-years as can be counted without foundering. We have been summoned, Kazantzakis said, and Shaw pronounced early on, to discover the impossible, the inexplicable, the cycles of rampant life here and on worlds so far distant we shall never know them. Notwithstanding, we dream them in our fictions and go a-traveling *up*. We are the beginners. We are beholden. Tens of millions were born and died before us. They are a sweet burden that we must carry into Space. Our destiny was born on the day the primitive eye was invented in the merest animal specule and began to see, examine, and one day realize that stuff in the sky, that mystery of stars.

In our new and spectacular age, we witness the growth of Space Travel at Canaveral, lift off our desires from gantries three hundred feet tall, proper straitjackets for *King Kong*, gun carriages to be fired against Time, Distance, and Ignorance. Shaw would have vacationed there to tonic up his spirits. Imagine him striding the Florida sands, interviewing astronauts but hearing himself as they replied.

At almost the same instant of our lunar landings, electronic brains fell among us to melt down from huge houses, rooms, then cubicles and closets to lap and wrist size. Gary Kasparov won out over a computerized chess player, thus scoring a victory for mankind? Bosh. Sniveling bosh. Shaw would have been the first to write a curtain raiser in which the computer is convicted of fraud, for as we all know, it was not a single machine that faced Kasparov but the intellectual guts of three dozen men who peed their brightness into the nerve endings of the Dumb Player. The computer only *looks* like a machine. It is the neuron endings, gastric juices, lifeblood, sweat, and ganglion fire that hide within, masking its stuffs with wires, fused by ten thousand instant welds.

I have never wondered at such. Visiting Apple Computer or any other electronic-gizmo works, when the tour guides said, "Isn't that wonderful?" I cried, "No!" Shocked, they asked me what I meant. "I mean," said I, "*it* is not wonderful. *You* are wonderful. You dreamed it. You blueprinted it. You built it. You infused it with process, with dream, with electronic imagination. It does not know it exists. You exist. You are the god I worship. A computer cannot best Kasparov. A legion of flesh-and-blood brains hid in a computer might. All hail Kasparov, all hail Apple battalions."

Man is, after all, the ghost in the contrivance. The lift under the wing of our aircraft is not miraculous; it is man who raises the airplane by discovering the invisible presence of "lift." Man makes visible all the unseen and contrives to make it palpable. With the X-ray and the microscope, Mankind blew the cover on death's-head skeletons closeted in living flesh. Bacterial annihilators were then reined in and destroyed for the first time in the history of our Earth.

All of these inventions would have been Life Force invigorators for Shaw. With the laptop computer as Moses' tablet, Shaw would have hyperventilated the modern stage, strutting his soul and outwriting Wells and all of us.

To Wells, whose last book was the sad *Mind at the End of Its Tether*, Shaw would have cried, "Sit, Herbert George, be still! Your tether laps the world, encircles Saturn, to unravel beyond Alpha Centauri. There *is* no end, but only an eternal Beginning. My behavior, as example, guarantees it. Melancholy entombs itself. Pessimism is a self-fulfilling prophecy. Let Canaveral be a New Year's Eve Fourth of July. Let all the rusted gantries jump alive with liquid oxygen-hydrogen fire. Let each gantry be a Christmas tree, decorated with life aloft to Anywhere But Here. Dear Herbert George, *Hamlet* may very well start with tombs and ghosts, proceed with skulls and graves, end with suicides and murder, but *I* write me a *new* text, H.G., not from tomb to tomb, death to death, but launch pad to launch pad, rockets shouting fire, men shouting a joyful rage against unknowingness. Come, H.G., shed that despair, Canaveral is the kindergarten of Time, Evolution, and Immortality. Don't spoil it. Don this silly helmet, blow this horn. Run, leaving your footprints to be blown away with the firewind as the last rocket targets the great Cosmic wall."

Shaw, as I have said, alive today, would dare to instruct gravity, admonish Congress, reprimand the do-nothings and the know-everythings-who-profess-nothing, then nest himself in a missile to be fired up and outrace all light-year spacecraft, shouting along the way, "If I am not the Holy Ghost, *who* is?" To which we, following, would respond, "If you're not God, along the way you'll do."

Speaking thus, of Shaw and science fiction, we must then bring up, with thunderous timpani and a battalion of brass, Hector Berlioz, whose *Symphonie Fantastique* might as well have been Symphony Future Incredible. For it was Berlioz who was not only a fine short-story writer but a great autobiographer, who made a rare headlong dash into the future with his "Euphonia, or the Musical City," which appears in his amazing *Evenings with the Orchestra*. In this story he imagined a town in 2344, whose inhabitants, every one, played or sang or acted music or experimented with acoustics and sound.

Well, then, what of this? I propose that we eject Shaw from

his grave to collide in midair with a similarly projectiled Berlioz over the Florida Space Life Preserve, to root them by the nearest abandoned gantry, to there relight that great tree with celebratory notes and festive fires. There Berlioz would compose the architecture of his "Euphonia" and conduct it on the fiery turf at sunset on the night of going away, a symphony of departure and arrival, to depart the gravities of Earth, to accept the centrifuges of the planets so they might whirl us on out to the final arrival: Alpha Centauri, where the immortality of man, as promised, predicted, and outlined by GBS the mountebank, will achieve its procreation and assurance. If the soul's heart and blood of Methuselah does not circumnavigate this, I will discard my intuition to be dry-cleaned.

The imagination of man is the promise of our flesh and blood delivered to far worlds. Not just by fitness or experimentation but by wild desire, incredible need, fantastic dream. Not by unfit accidents but by waking intuition, blueprint, construction, and culmination.

Berlioz and Shaw conjoined could let Shaw write treatise, lyric, and prologue, then double in cymbal and lunar drum, and on occasion elbow Berlioz off the podium to pound the orchestra into submission, then leap off to sit as audience and caper his pen to criticize composer, choirs, as well as the Man with the Gunshot Beard lurking with his brass. From there Shaw might vault to the nearest planetarium to advise Cosmos and God, the whole dominion, on all planetary arousals and diminishments.

So on the vast stage of Cosmic History, that stage whisper overheard will rise from the prompter's nest where GBS, stashed, could choreograph Moses with an empty tablet, Christ poised to vanish from the tomb as a great illusion, and the Big Bang theory shown as pipsqueak popgun nonevent.

Can this be done? With careful planning now we can fuse

Shaw and Berlioz on the Florida dunes just beyond 2001. They are, after all, the founders of Awe. The young cubs Spielberg, Lucas, and Kubrick are merely promoters. They did not engender the Universe. Shaw swam over the whole damned spread to seed the Cosmic eggs. With his Methuselah brain outliving his body, he was an entire committee, which created not that infamous camel but a Lamarckian giraffe.

Whose neck, look there, will never stop growing!

ABOUT LIFE

THE BEAUTIFUL BAD WEATHER (2000)

The advertisements entice us with serene tidal waters, clear skies, philosophical perambulations along shores where the breeze whispers, strange birds cry, plus there are dreamless siestas after good food, fine wines.

But I preach wind and rain, El Greco skies storm-lit by lightnings, thunders to break the bones, and museums and country houses evacuated by storms where fortunate tourists wander unmolested and alone.

Do you profess, you say, glancing out your London or Rome window, finding a multitudinous drench of rain, and plunging out in it? Would you have us dance partners with lightning and seek shelter at Tivoli where it rains both ways?

I would.

Not mad dogs and Englishmen gone out in the noonday sun. But tourists surprised by the joy lodged in weather, lacking umbrellas and raising their faces to be washed clean as God's children, daring to launch themselves midstream at Blenheim or midgarden at Hadrian's Villa.

Most travelers, having promised themselves ten days of full sunlight, less shadow, recoil like salted snails, grousing, at the first bank of fog, the least drizzle.

Not I. Not me. And, thank God, not my wife.

We are kin to downpours in Ireland, Italy, and England.

Ireland first.

Ireland, where it rains forty-five days a month. How the hell they cram that into their bleak calendar, I cannot say. I only know it's done.

It was there that I first learned the beauty of the incessant storm.

I was there to work for Ahab's clone, John Huston, seeking to harpoon *Moby Dick*, breaching, with a screenplay through his heart. Lodged in the Royal Hibernian Hotel, I spent six months hunchbacking my typewriter, as the winter sun vanished at 3:00 P.M., casting my eye at the weeping windows to hear the thunders echo Melville.

"If it's weather you want," said the front doorman of the Royal Hibernian, "down there's the river Liffey and O'Connell Bridge, where all the rain goes. You'll be a drowned rat. You're not *really* going out in all this?"

I glanced at the dark-night theater of storms.

"It seems I am," I said.

"God loves your kind," he said.

"What kind is that?"

"Simple." He opened the door to let in the night and let out the daft.

With the rain banging my face, I yanked my cap down and thought, Why am I *doing* this?

"Because."

Which is the best reason for writers to go a-journeying.

I walked through the rain and then strode through the rain, and the more I walked, the more I developed an appetite for weather. The rain, banging my shoulders, turned me this way, that, around, and back in an exhilaration so wild I laughed at my own lunacy. Stop! I thought. Buy a brandy. Go to bed. No, no! Where's the Yeats statue, the theater, the Liffey Bridge? I went.

To find what? Beggars in front of hotels large and small, hands up palming the rain for coins. An old woman strumming a harp half out of the pour, pringling her fingers through harp strings and beaded curtains of rain, with music between. Then a swift run past pubs where sheepfolds of men, glued close by taunts and gibes, ignored the drench, remembered their wives, and begged another round; and thence to the Gaiety Theatre porch, where a tinker of taffy broke it with a silver hammer, minding the exit, for if the play were shopworn, some ticket holders might escape between scenes to buy sweets heading home; and thence on to the Shelborne Hotel, where a shawl-wrapped woman thrust forth a swaddled babe asking God and the hotel tenants to see his despair, his unwiped nose, buy him a bun and her: warm gin. And later in my jog around Dublin, at another hotel the same babe uplifted by a different ma, the babe borrowed from hand to hand, hotel to hotel, clocking long hours for insufficient pay. And back on O'Connell Bridge, where one beggar stood, head bared, no cap, the drizzle drumming his pate and him singing "Devil Take the Brits" if he thought you one, or "Sweet Molly Malone" if he saw Boston in your gait. I passed him many wild nights till he vanished. They said he hurled his accordion into the Liffey and jumped after to be lost. But they said later it was his accordion drowned and himself, Guinness-soaked, found curbside weeks on.

Coming alone, I ran alone and left alone.

The drowned rat came back to a warm hotel for a hot Irish coffee to find the kitchen help in mutiny against the French chef.

So that's Dublin, the river, the bridge, the beggars, and this rain stalker.

So when did my wife start to relish the lovely foul weathers?

Italy, Rome, Tivoli.

Tivoli and its garden fountains cascading skyward, rushing in waterfalls or jetting from stone goddesses' breasts.

Tivoli and myself and wife and daughters, stepping through the waterworks garden on an undecided day . . .

When final decisions were made. The clouds let go.

"Hey, we didn't know," my daughters cried, "there were so *many* fountains!"

"There aren't," I said. "Those going up are manmade. Those coming down, God-given."

And it was true. In glorious unison the Tivoli sprays and jets and arcs met ten thousand string beads hammering down. Fount met fount in beautiful collisions, and us few wandering between, happy as Christmas dogs.

All those gods afrolic in the Fontana di Trevi never had it so good.

I glanced back at two buses crammed with huddled tourist masses, fearful of storms. I could read their lips:

"Look at that crazy man and his family. What are they *doing* in there?"

I lifted my face and gargled rain.

And yet again: Rome, late night, dawn still beyond the hills. Dogs and cats asleep in the Colosseum. Motorbikes exhausted from late parties, dead. No creatures stirring. Mist in the air, fog in the alleys. No time for tourists. But still . . .

Sleepless at 5:00 A.M., chewing the travel metaphors behind my eyeballs, I rose to lean out the window of the Hotel Hassler.

Shadows and darkness. A dim ghost shape far off: St. Peter's.

But below I saw a single yellow light in the courtyard. A lone taxi with an optimistic driver ready to jump should a crazed American choose this wrong hour for no reason.

Me.

Yes. No. Yes. No.

Do it! I said. This won't happen again! Pull on your tennis shorts and—

Go!

The taxi driver was shocked to see a sleepwalker lurch at him saying, "You available?"

The driver looked at his cab with doubt.

I jumped into the backseat.

"Where?" he said.

"There's only *one* place."

"Ah, yes," he said, and stripped the gears, rocketed down dark alleys, and arrived us breathless, by the big phantom façade jailed in the Bernini pillar ghosts.

The Basilica of St. Peter.

"There's nothing to see," he said.

"Wait," I whispered.

And the sun rose.

Not much. The merest thread of fire on the eastern slopes. And then another thread and another of immense flame that made the shadows melt from the great façade, and the entire basilica was bathed in orange-pink light, and the windows flashed like gold war shields, and I slid from the car quietly to steal the moment and stood in the middle of the square by the Egyptian obelisk, alone, alone, beautifully alone, no humans in sight, and just the taxi near, and silence.

Oh, God, I thought, tears filling my eyes. Rome is mine. I *own* the whole damn place!

And I did, I did. For a minute, two minutes, three, as the sunlight lowered itself down and down the basilica and warmed the vast marble to a great hearth. Soon the bells of a hundred churches across Rome and its ruins would ring, and life would rise and nuns and priests arrive, followed by the faithful.

But for now, imprisoned by Bernini, stunned by this mountain reared by Michelangelo, I knew no words. Then, suddenly, I ran a few steps and shouted up at John Paul's window.

"*Papa*," I cried. "God bless you!"

Blushing, I shut up.

Quiet applause. My driver, smiling, moved his hands softly.

He repeated my call in Italian.

I stood, hating to leave.

But the weather was changing, the cold gone, and all that winter stone was warm flesh.

Rome's bells chimed.

I found the car blindly and did not look back as we drove away.

Then our most wonderful encounter with miserably fine weather came in London soon after. Eating breakfast in our hotel room, Maggie and I chatted up our expedition that day to Oxford and Blenheim, the great marble spread where Churchill was born resembling his later self, one hour old. A great flash of lightning followed by a Beethoven thunderclap informed us that our routine might suffer change.

At the window we saw a city in half flood and a sky intemperate with clouds and scarred by lightning.

"Well," said Maggie, "there goes our day."

"No!" I cried. "On with your raincoat. We're off."

"Where?"

"Blenheim," I said. "In a twenty-four-hour unceasing rain."

And Blenheim it was, and rain it did.

To Blenheim Palace, home of Lord Randolph, Churchill's ancestor.

We wandered the flagged halls and marble solitudes, solitary ourselves, preserving the silence, letting the great winepress of weather crush the monumental halls and wings, and we arrived at a huge tapestry portraying the victory at Blenheim by Lord Randolph with great fiery blossoms of gunfire, troops asprint, cannons widemouthed with victory. And as we stared, the peak of the storm arrived in ruination. Lightning banged the porches outside the windows. Thunderclaps followed in midgasp. A Beethoven cannonade, but there was no need for Ludwig's quakes—the countryside shook, Blenheim gave answer in every timber and beam. The mosaics beneath threatened to erupt in new metaphors. Maggie and I stood before the rampant troops eager for life or proper deaths, and all the late-afternoon lights died, and candles were lit to refire the charge, and by the time Maggie and I came forth, concussed by guns and now concussed by rain, we knew that we, not Churchill's lord, had run, leaped, and fought to win Blenheim, win Blenheim again anytime new storms came to refire history.

We drove away in the rain.

But now a final good meteorological report.

Arriving in Paris each summer, it is my custom, traveling to my hotel, to leap from my car, rush out on the broad esplanade of the Trocadéro overlooking the Eiffel Tower and all Paris, lift my arms, and shout:

"Paris, I'm here!"

And, leaving two weeks later, follow the same routine, but quieter:

"Paris, good-bye."

On my last visit, it was raining great skyfuls. I jumped out at the Trocadéro and started to run when my driver brandished an umbrella.

"No, no!" I cried, waving him off. "Don't you understand? I *want* to get wet!"

THE AFFLUENCE OF DESPAIR:
AMERICA THROUGH THE LOOKING GLASS (1998)

How come?

How come we're one of the greatest nations in the world . . .

And yet this feeling of doom?

How come, while our president walks wounded, we ourselves jog along nicely, but . . .

Under a dark cloud that says something awful is about to happen?

How come, with five hundred thousand immigrants a year yammering to flood in . . .

We enjoy what I describe as the Affluence of Despair?

How come?

Who has not, as a child, rushed to the mirror to find one's face, mouth, eyes, thinking, I *must* see myself in full flood? Quick, before the sorrow melts!

America today.

I wonder how I look this hour, what I feel this minute, what I'm imagining *now*.

So TV switch: ON!

We have met the enemy, and it is us.

We celebrate ourselves. Right, Walt Whitman?

We run in terror from . . . our shadows. Yes, Mr. Poe?

Orwell, listen up:

Not Big Brother above our kitchen sinks.

But big sister, mother, uncle, sibling, family vaudeville—
Us.

Not things but *we* are in the saddle and ride mankind. Both horse and rider, we win, place, and show at the mirror maze local TV news window. The soul that rakes the cash betting against ourselves is, once again—

I. Me. Myself.

We.

We contrive habits, fork over moola, inhale poisons, catch nicotine colds, cough out our lungs, pretend we are not responsible, and, outraged, sue . . .

Two hundred fifty million innocent people.

Us.

And pay out billions to second-smoke lawyers to drag us into court, pretending we are not guilty, it is those leaf growers over there. Yeah!

Them.

Help me rend my clothes, tear my hair, acid-rinse my X-rays. Meanwhile, how do I look in the housefly 80-million-lensed TV eye on lightning striking America the Beautiful? Did you catch me last night confessing what I caught and what caught me?

Recall Starbuck's advice to mad Ahab?

Do not fear me, old man. Beware of thy self, *my captain.*

America, now hear this. Beware of thyself. The day of judgment will not arrive; it's already here. We judge and doom ourselves. We the murderers and we the victims, we the funeral managers and ourselves boxed in the grave.

In Orwell's urban prison, Big Brother glared from every ceiling.

Today *we* are everywhere *loving* to be watched. Not Big Brother the smiler with the wide-screen knife, but, my God, look, *I* am on channel 9!

The problem is not Stalin's ghost, but *we* prevail, displayed in the biggest damn football, baseball, basketball game in history.

We do not suffer from totalitarian lunatics but from the astonishing proliferation of our images that weep in our potato-bin parlors and TV-sales storefronts, where we can view our own faces cloned ninety times on showroom screens.

We perform for us, not Big Brother. We have fallen in love with mirrors. Flash a camera and your merest broccoli-headed citizen morphs to Travolta or Madonna.

And all of it on local TV news, in fifteen-second disaster updates. Breaking bones, breaking news, at eleven. "Tell us, Mrs. Gutierrez, how's it feel with your son shotgunned minutes ago?"

We do not go to the theater; we *are* the theater. We knock Godzilla aside to ascend his throne.

We have invaded the TV studios and run the country to mania on big-time talking-head shows. We display our factoid brilliance on *Jeopardy!*, forgetting that its factoids are 90 percent useless once you kill the set. We don't ask *who* Napoleon was, but *where* buried. Or not *why* he invaded Russia, but *when*.

In sum, we wear our hearts on our sleaze.

A friend of mine bragged he had bought a dish that could cup, cull, and catch two hundred—count 'em, two hundred—channels raining across a moron sky.

Hell, I said, you've just got a bigger windmill to catch two hundred tons of horse puckey, bull dung, and rabbit pellets.

It all hits the fan every night, a year of O.J. blood manure here, ten years of House of Usher AIDS there, the killing fields of American high roads just beyond, each car a glorious pyre to mindless speed, and in every front yard a Mrs. Gutierrez questioned but watching the TV mirror to see how she plays.

As a character in *Bridge on the River Kwai* once cried: Madness!

Those epileptic souls at football, baseball, hockey matches, who frenzy for the TV camera, how decimate their pantomimes, shut their laughter?

How?

With Medusa watching, not freezing but freeing you to shriek, Yeah Team!

And the Team is Us. We.

We the judges and jurors trying, damning, or freeing the guilty, weighing topics we're unqualified to answer. How to cork this motormouth diarrhea?

The problem is not with our national full-coverage news, which can be mildly depressing. It is with the assault of your local TV paparazzi who machine-gun you with forty decapitations, sexual harassments, gangster executions, in fifteen-second explosions for the full half hour. Is there nothing we cannot wipe our pigpen hands on? Is there a woman so pure we cannot silt her underwear, a man so bright we cannot blind his sun? Sound bite: mass suicides. Photos at eleven. No attack army could survive that fusillade. Bullets, real and psychological, wound and kill.

So we must stand alert to our central core despair, targeting our Panic of the Week syndrome, mostly a local TV news séance.

Every week, fifty-two weeks a year, they need a prime disaster focus, to spin the garbage and glue the potato people to the tube.

Remember the Alar-poisoned apples that the dinnertime news bites claimed would destroy us, so they destroyed some part of the apple industry? Panic.

Recall the poison cellar gas rising to asphyxiate your kids? More panic.

Or those arsenic-filled Peruvian grapes promising to strip our gears.

Or the Three Mile Island nuclear meltdown where nothing melted, no injuries, no deaths.

Panic for two weeks, make it three. Ratings up. Morale down. Not to mention O.J. for breakfast, lunch, and dinner. By the panic-oriented week? No, the year!

What to do?

The old Civil War song says it:

Look away, look away, look away, Dixieland.

Is it that simple? Is then the only solution to "look away"?

For starters, in a democratic zoo with us as the keepers and the kept, yes.

Look away, chop the TV local news on the hour or half hour.

Leave a message on your local station's machine, describing their stupidity.

If you meet their newsreaders, male or female, tell them that they are overpaid and underbrained. Ask them if it would be too much trouble to air twenty-second news bites instead of fifteen-second flashes. *Think* of the extra enrichment!

If you can't tell them, join the Internet. It's your turn to blather.

Will this work? Perhaps. The Man Without a Country died of social deprivation. Stop saying that these TV hookers are high-class thinkers; they're mere graffiti bums, not Einstein's by-blows. Ask them to give back their fortunes and hand us real news.

I remember Saul Bass when he redesigned the Bell Telephone service vans years ago in clean bright blues and whites. The repairmen fought the change. It was too pretty, they said.

What to do? How to get the telephone workers to drive the new vans? Bass instructed his three dozen artists to wander the city. Each time they saw a bright new blue-and-white telephone van, they must shout at the driver: "Hey, nice car!" "Looks *grrreat*!" "Wish I had a van like *that*!"

Dumb, right? Wrong. It worked. In a month the Bell repairmen were bragging on their vans and driving proud.

So instead of treating chat-show hosts as Cinderellas, tell them they are ugly sisters whose lips spew not diamonds and emeralds but spiders, frogs, and toads; each time they open their mouths, they spoil the ecology. Hand them some Lifebuoy. Tell them to chew.

The bottom line is, if you stare like stunned deer in midroad, blinded by the lights that rush to run you down, you must expect that a thousand and one such nights in such a brutal harem will convince you that the end of the world is at hand, that America is bestial, and that suicide, murder, rape, and AIDS are the fashion of the day.

We must, then, speak to these confessors of our dark souls and tell them that their awful truths in awesome repetition ends with the Big Lie. We are not as bad as they say we are, but we feel this despair because they have somehow proved that the razored wrist is our metaphor and the slit throat a lesson in linguistics.

Will all this make the local TV pundits pull up their socks and uncrick the hunch in their backs? They might begin to commence. We don't ask for Pollyanna reruns, but just a tad of balance. Some spearmint gum with the arsenic. Some rejuvenating trampoline with the roadkill. Some hang glider with the deadfall.

For starters, when some good-guy celebrity dies, bury him in fifty-nine seconds instead of ten. Linger a long trifle, as against a mindless brush-off.

Meanwhile, we can permit ourselves to watch Jim Lehrer,

George Will, Sam Donaldson, and Cokie Roberts, who are intelligent, informative, and, in the main, nonpolitical coast-to-coast.

The McLaughlin Gang, also, if we can *understand* them.

From time to time, then, we must brush our teeth and run not to glance in mirrors at our crock of tears but to cloud that mirror with our fresh breath, then turn to find a real mirror and rediscover ourselves.

Yes, we have met the enemy, and they are us. . . .

But also, traveling from village to town to city across our continental spread, have we not met the friendly Indians: Italian, Swedish, Spanish, and old English-German?

And are they not, also, Us?

They are.

We have condemned ourselves. Now we must save ourselves. No one else can. Shut off the set. Write your local TV newspeople. Tell them to go to hell. Take a shower. Go sit on the lawn with friends.

THE HUNCHBACK, THE PHANTOM, THE MUMMY, AND ME (UNDATED)

My favorite horror films have haunted my entire life. They have inhabited me so that when I wrote *A Graveyard for Lunatics* some years ago, *The Hunchback*, *The Phantom*, and *Kong* dominated the novel.

Why have these films lived on in me for seventy-seven years?

Obviously because they are stories about love. In some cases unrequited love: *The Hunchback* and *The Phantom*. And in the case of the Mummy, he comes to life seeking his dead Egyptian princess. With King Kong it's in the finale, when the character called Carl Denham says, "Oh, no, it was *Beauty* killed the Beast." So love is central. Consider the Bride of Frankenstein's search for love and the terror that ends the search. Two other fine examples of a special unrequited love are *The Man Who Could Work Miracles* and *The Invisible Man* by H. G. Wells. The metaphor in each is simple: The love of power, which as could easily be predicted, didn't love back but only corrupted.

When I was nineteen, selling newspapers on the street corner, with the very first money I made, I went to a recording studio in Hollywood and there ranted and raved one afternoon, playing out the roles of *The Invisible Man*, as done by the superb Claude Rains, and the hero of *The Man Who Could Work Miracles*, played by Roland Young. Both plays have to do with a kind of lunacy that occurs when men become tired of tolerating humanity and the universe. There's a hidden strain of this in most men that never comes out, but which is revealed to fine effect in these two pictures.

The second great truth about these films and later similar films is that they are pure metaphor. Simply, they declare a metaphor and dramatize it without complication. When a metaphor is acted out, it's easy to recall it in tranquillity outside the theater.

When I saw the Hunchback for the first time, I was three. It convinced me that there was something wrong with me. I was crushed down when I left the theater with my mother. Fifteen years later, I saw the film at the Filmart Theater in Hollywood and told my friends I remembered everything about it from the age of three. They laughed; nobody could possibly remember all that. I replied, Well, there's this scene and that scene and a third scene and a fourth and the finale goes like *this*! We went in to see *The Hunchback of Notre Dame*, and there were all the scenes that I remembered from 1923. Metaphor had done its work!

The problem with our latest horror films is that they think if one metaphor is good, then two dozen are superb.

The current version of *The Mummy* is a dumb example. If the original *Mummy* scared you with less as more, why not load up on bodies to prickle your spine? So many mummies hurl themselves at you, gibbering, that you laugh and cry, *What*? Am I such a fool as to take fright at a death battalion when one would suffice? And especially one that, hidden in shadow, is never seen moving? But these new mummies Saint Vitus–danced into the light, and millions paid money to laugh.

The old films were satisfied to give you brief glimpses of horror. *The Hunchback*, of course, is not a horror film at all but a tale of grotesquerie, immensely sad. With *The Phantom*, you have only one scene for a few seconds, when the Phantom, un-masked, rises to accuse his beloved.

Similarly, consider Boris Karloff in his sarcophagus when his eyes open and his hand falls to his sides. That's *all*.

Minutes later, when the Egyptologist is studying the papyrus, the hand of the Mummy takes the manuscript from the desk. The Egyptologist, in horror, looks off-screen, and all you ever see of the Mummy is a fragment of the wrappings that encased him being trailed along the floor by someone unseen. At the end the Mummy is destroyed in a mere six seconds of disintegration.

So there are your sublime examples of films that work because they dare to be subtle.

I argued this with Universal when I wrote *It Came from Outer Space*. In my original treatment, I was careful to indicate that the invaders from another world should be hidden in shadow. Universal chose to bring them out in the light. I protested, but they wouldn't listen. Very late in time now, you could wield some scissors, cut the seven seconds from the film that destroyed the illusion, and wind up with a very nice picture indeed. Those beasts that appeared, close up, were comedians not to be taken seriously.

A glorious example of a film that truly terrifies is *The Haunting*, directed by Robert Wise, made at MGM in 1962. Everything is shadow and lack of substance. Everything is ultimately a radio show; you hear much and see nothing. It manages to cause a permanent curvature of your spine.

I first saw *The Haunting* at a private screening with Robert Wise thirty-eight years ago.

My God, I thought, this film belongs at the top of the list with *Citizen Kane* and *The Magnificent Ambersons*.

My God, fool! I thought again, Robert Wise edited *Kane* and *Ambersons*—he's Orson Welles's bastard son.

My dearest hope is that he hasn't seen the new *Haunting*.

If he came from such a screening, he might well, looking down, discover that someone had peed on his Reeboks.

ANY FRIEND OF TRAINS IS A FRIEND OF MINE (1968)

There is a special moment for me, crossing the continental United States by train in the early hours of dusk, when I enter alone—and first—to the hushed dining car and stand gazing along the aisle of white linen and hear a very special sound:

The tintinnabulation of shiny silverware.

The multitudes of silvery chimes, the small touchings of a thousand knives, forks, spoons, swayed by the train's glide around an endless mountain curve, causing the tiny implements to nudge, tap, push, speak their bodies against themselves.

Train travel speaks to me as much in this voice as in the old churning smokes of lost engines or the great throb of our new diesels hauling fellow creatures and freights out of the yellow desert into the new green, up from the westering sun through the high cold of night on the plateaus of the Great Divide.

And, flashing by lonely way stations and deserted switchman's towers, there is always the feeling: You're trapped on a nonstop jet, you can't get off. But the free soul, yes, the soul that dares to change locomotive riverbeds for no reason, can pick and choose from the always arriving, always departing towns. Then, in wild impulse, get off the train to admire strangeness and welcome surprise.

You haven't done it often. You may never do it again. But the imagination says: Could be.

This afternoon late. Tomorrow morning early. In a place you

never imagined but now will remember forever, step out in wilderness halfway between Tonopah and Buffalo Tread.

And the land is there as it was two hundred years ago, the same, unchanged—the raw land, waiting with an immense and unblinking stare. And you, no better than an astronaut delivered forth to alien planets, far out on the rim of Montana or Colorado or alone like a single stalk of Indian corn on the spread-flat Kansas prairie.

Remember when *Mariner 4* flashed photos back from Mars and people cried, No one there! Mars is dead!

But the astronauts, four hundred miles high, camera-shooting our own earth, have captured no life, no stir of civilization either.

And at forty thousand feet, in a continent-crossing jet, the facts are about the same.

We fly high, see nothing, and yet wonder at our alienation.

Give me the train, then, so I can see and know and truly feel and be stirred by the history of our people.

For a few short hours out of a busy life, let me really believe we did it all.

By private automobile one is tempted to do the American thing—fly before fury, think, at eighty miles per hour, of destinations instead of environments to be lingered on, noticed, and filed away with some leisure.

For, riding the train, you build the roads, rear the farms, till the fields, chop the wood fences, pile the rocks in walls, push back the night, light lamps in lonely cottages, and suddenly bang together full towns and cities and stand back and be touched and know pride in it all.

I have, myself, built this country thirty or forty times in my life. Because of the train, I have pathfound the maps of this nation's beginning and middle life, which are as familiar as the roadways on the palm of my hand.

I have got off trains in a hundred jerkwater (once they jerked a rope to let the water from the big wooden water tanks thunder down into the old steam-engine boiler), I say, jerkwater towns and time-worn cities across our land, where we changed engines or waited for other trains to pass through. I have watched my dusty footprints blown away behind me in Texas streets so far from Amarillo I can't tell you. And I have walked through the streets of Cheyenne, feeling like some mute New England farm boy, soft as butter, lost among men who strode shadowed by their Stetsons—all bone, gristle, sinew, tendon, and jerky beef, forever married to the horse and friend to that wind that leaves no sign where they have passed.

My earliest memories are those of trains . . .

My brother and I, hiking every summer along the main line out of Waukegan, Illinois, amid the smell of wood ties, black tar, and urine laid down in a wild rain from the Milwaukee express, kneeling at noon to place our ears on the sun-blasted rails, frying our peach-fuzz cheeks to hear the fast approach of the train storming south out of Wisconsin.

Or the five-o'clock-in-the-morning train that pulled in down by the empty lake shore. My brother and I up early, shouting in whispers, dressing as we ran across town to stand and watch the circus elephants unload in the cold dark. And all the animals in their night-barred cages shivering their hides, horses jingling their black-and-silver equipments, men cursing, lions roaring, the camels, zebras, llamas passing in a dawn line—the mighty burden of Barnum's entertainments opening out and unfolding from the mile-long freights . . . a memory to be kept all one's life.

My wife, not long ago, flew to New York with two of our daughters. She reported later that America was a Jerry Lewis–Elvis Presley Festival, hard to ignore at an altitude of forty thousand feet.

Meanwhile, on Earth, back in Kansas by night, snug on a train, my other two daughters and I stayed up almost until dawn. Why? Because, rolling along, a series of bright flashes ahead made us think we were approaching a war-games area, a field of some strange artilleries exploding bright battles in a cloudy night. And then we found to our amazement that our train was moving upon and then in and through a July storm of lightning and thunder. Vast bolts plunged earthward all about us as we huddled, nestled to the window, noses pressed to the glass, safe despite the downrush of light and sound. And if our train were to be hit, what of that? We could take all the bolts God delivered, devour them whole, and flush them through the always coming, always going rails.

So the night went, the train gliding among stilts of fire, huge laboratory experiments of electric flame, then rumbling coughs of thunder as great blind hands of shocked air clapped tight, the night's echoing applause for its own bright words.

On other trains, at other times, in other late-night hours, I have communed with George Bernard Shaw, G. K. Chesterton, and Charlie Dickens—old cronies who go with me everywhere, unseen but felt, silent but in continuous uproar. We carouse to all hours in the dining car or the club car or the reading vestibule and make converse with any idea tossed in the air.

Sometimes Aldous Huxley sits in with us, blind and wandering-wise. Richard III has gone with me often, prating the virtues of murder. Half across Kansas I have buried Caesar in the middle of the night, Antony giving his oration as we steamed out of Elderberry Springs.

The books I always wanted to read, the plays I always wanted to write, I read and write on trains.

But most of all, trains are a time for Bernard and G.K. and Charlie and Aldous to talk, and for me to listen.

This year, probably more than any recent year, the American soul is in need of religious retreats. And is not the train one of the last, and perhaps most logical, places where we can satisfy our terrible hunger to get away?

Is it too much to ask of the coast-to-coast-voyaging American, who always pleads the excuse of time, to perhaps once a year place himself for two and one-half short days in an environment where he cannot use telephones and, best of all, where the barracuda telephone cannot devour him? Are sixty hours too many to give for what one receives back from such a journey?

Or, as some suspect, are we afraid to be alone with ourselves? Are we like those celebrities we cluck our tongues over—who surround themselves with eternal partyings, jesters, pranksters, noisemakers, babblers, and honkers? Somewhere mustn't the party hold its breath for one moment of silence? Sometime mustn't we, crossing Oklahoma as the sun rises, know the beauty and the dread in that moment of self-revelation when we look in the small train mirror, shaving, after a night of watching the high, bright stars wheel over the sky, and think, Who am I? What? Where am I? Where going and why? To what good purpose or what bad end? And whither fleeing?

Mustn't we touch the scales to weigh our friends, list enemies (among them, surely at times, our own name), and, alone, a single person, away from family, speak the names of those we truly love, the names of our children, wives, husbands, the names of a few solitaries, those friends we do trust toward the middle of a life now clear, now somewhat confused?

So it is the silence, and the serenity, and the peace, plus some small terror and the dread chance for self-conversation that lures me back to the train. The unblinking regard and full stare of that fellow in the mirror, shaving at dawn or waiting to shave before the eventide meal, I go there to meet him.

It follows, then, that if there were no trains—and someday soon they may be gone—we would have to reinvent them or something like them. Rip up the tracks of such traveling self-confessionals, only to lay them again at some future date, to be used by such homespun sinners as I, naming myself as destination.

The jet knows only two places—where it takes off and where it lands. It is like the swift freeways of Los Angeles, rolling through Watts, ignorant of its existence.

I must choose trains in order to allow myself time to relate to that earth and the men who changed it, just a few feet outside my window in the passing weathers.

And finally, in so traveling, I like the certain, sure, the positive feeling that comes with seeing all the small houses go by in the night, swing by in the dark, glide by in the huge spread of fields. It is then that I think, By God, now, the silhouettes on those porches, the kids in those swings late of summer evenings, the men smoking on front steps, the souls behind the lit windows—all those people, all, all, all those people, damn it to hell—they just can't all be unhappy. They are not all doomed. They are not all dreadful, sick, not all in dire and awful straits.

Poor some of them, yes; black some of them, yes; Indian and Mexican some of them, yes; holding on by their teeth and guts and will to the dust-blowing edge of mesas or the junk-strewn back lots of towns that look like deserted film sets.

I know, I know. I do not for a minute forget the dark gusts that roll dooms like tumbleweeds in the night across troubled

America. But for a few hours on a few days, at least I see the mixture. I know the paradox of this country. Like that pitcher of water—described by doomsters as half empty and by Polly-annas as half full—we are neither half mad nor half sane, but best spoken of as some wild place between: a fabulous, ram-shackle concoction of peoples, places, times, and journeys that somehow, in some lump-wheeled manner of fashion, stays on the tracks, reaches where it wants, and comes back for another go-round.

And as the small towns swing by, arc by, wheel by in the night, lit and unlit, lonely and warm, sleeping sound or sitting up late with some hidden pain, I read their lives with one sweep from my traveling window and—sensing, believing—wish them well.

Good people, mostly good people, people neither too happy nor too unhappy . . . there they curve off over the earth.

And at each lone station, I sling out some part of my soul for those snatch-away mail grabs. And even as some parcel or packet of letters is seized by the flailing hook in the dark and empty station at three in the morning and is saved there for opening at sunrise, so some part of me is snatched and kept in those towns. And in equal part, I glean some portion of the mixture, the fabulous collaboration of pinings-away and re-vivals, the wakes and the weddings. I see, feel, know, touch—by reading the signs that vanish in the hills.

The train, with a sound not unlike the sound of the wild herds at night on the plains a hundred years ago, moves on. With the look of the bison, the proud hunched profile of the buffalo, the train plows the fields of fresh-made morning.

So I go with it. I would not dream to be left behind.

I'M MAD AS HELL, AND I'M NOT GOING TO TAKE IT ANYMORE! (THE NEW MILLENNIUM, THAT IS) (UNDATED)

Forgive my borrowing Peter Finch's cry in *Network*.

But I *am* mad as hell.

Because on December 31, 1999, a mob of gullible freaks will douse their tonsils and jubilate their bods shouting, "Happy twenty-first century!"

A half billion champagne cocktails will drown these dimwits cramming hotels in Paris, New York, and Las Vegas to speed the New Millennium, their wives ripe with the first twenty-first-century babes.

Damn!

I've preached to the maniac ostriches all year. But, heads sunk in millennial sand, they pop more corks and bake more embryos.

Now hear this:

Stash the confetti. Recoil the ticker tape. Eiffel Tower, kill those mile-high numbers counting down to 2000. Millennial Santa just crashed with an empty sack.

And while you caution your eager embryo to tread water another year, here are my predictions for the *real* New Year's, January 1, 2001.

Once I asked Edith Head, Hollywood's foremost costume designer, to predict the future.

"In 2033," I said, "how will men and women dress?"

"No," she said. "If I promise fashions, they *happen*. Tomorrow arrives by noon today, and you must start over, imagining the impossible."

"Just *guessing* causes an instant Tomorrow?"

"We imagined the Moon, didn't we? And *Eagle* landed. We wished for Mars; the Viking cameras followed. So predictions *ensure*. What do you *want* from the Universe? Dream, then shout it loud and clear or there will *be* no new New Years. But watch it! You may get what you shout."

I dare to shout our future now.

First we must wish ourselves back to the Moon.

We should never have aborted its not so wild a dream.

There we must build space stations on hard lunar rock, escaping the gravities of raw space. Why? More of this later.

Meanwhile . . .

In the first hundred years of the third millennium, several dozen new universities will be added to our educational rosters. Let's name a few. The University of Sing Sing. The Campus of the Illinois Penitentiary, San Quentin College, and Alcatraz U.

Strange?

Strange, yes, because new.

Beyond 2001 we will learn what we should always have known: Punishment is not enough.

Repentance through education might suffice.

By the gate of each penal school, we will retranslate the Statue of Liberty's demand: Give me your vacant minds and useless passions, lend me your rootless self-destroyers, let all books be Bibles, in monks' cells, where the study of mankind will prevail.

And when these empty heads are full and these brutal hands can write, let there be tests, and for those that at last can read, remember, and understand what they read, let the portals open to set them free, punished but replenished, on their feet, not on their knees.

And those who have not studied, learned, remembered, and thought, let them stay for rereplenishment. Prisons that are schools, schools that drain the poisons and refit the psyches. Let Lazarus come forth more than reborn, truly alive.

With more learning, more good behavior, time off. Increased minds, reduced sentences.

It's worth a try.

And now, oh, Lord, a further wish and hoped-for resolution. Let all the nations and cities of the world for a little while be governed by women. We have ingested testosterone from the mouth of the cave to the burned libraries of Alexandria to unending world wars. Even as men are lousy drivers (check your insurance statistics), so they are lousy politicos who, guarding their ravenous egos, ignore their teeming brains. Not back of the bus for men, no, but as side-seat advisers on how to get lost. For a few years, why not? Let women "man" the wheel.

And, please, no women who are macho-male clones with incipient biceps. Just ordinary, which means extraordinary, females who can mother-nurse-teach the world, with all that those labels imply. Men, confronted by problems, often depart. Women stay to sort baggage, clean souls, and mend tempers.

Which is a natural lead-in to computers, the Internet, e-mail, and wide-screen wall-to-wall eyeball TV. The world I depicted in *Fahrenheit 451* way back in 1951 is fast targeting ground zero, not like an express train but a brain-meltdown rocket. Women must make a takeover power grab, because men-who-would-be-boys are now bigger boys with bigger toys. The virtual realists invade us, and if Bill Gates isn't Big Brother, he is a distant subliminal cousin. We are being urged to transistorize our entire household with factoid basement kindergartens and empty high-school attics that graduate students with comic-strip diplomas.

Speaking at a local library last year, I saw that Bill Gates had signed in the guest book. Under his name I wrote, "*I don't do Windows.*"

How come this fuddy-duddy neo-Luddite reaction?

Aren't I supposed to be a true inhabitant of the Future, born on Mars, flung from Saturn's rings, flying ahead of the saucers?

True. I am H. G. Wells's bastard son, out of Mary Wollstonecraft Shelley. Which means I truly believe in a future, while the Internet people stay late maundering and whimpering to morons in Moscow and lunatics in Louisiana. Your modern macho male, who reminds me of Laocoön, that Herculean marble god wrestling a giant snake. Today's electronic male is enmeshed with his genitalia, fighting for freedom to be lost on the Internet. Millions of calls per hour crisscross continents, sent and received by forty-two-year-old boy mechanics eager to trade vacuum tubes and dead transistors with similar boobs in Bangkok and Barcelona. Well, at least it keeps them out of harm's way, giving the grand chance for the women to seize power, while the giant kid's midlife frenzy broadcasts hot-air cartoon balloons pacing Telstar to land on fallow ground.

My response: Turn off everything. Patrol your house to pull the plugs on the TV, the radio, the fax, the e-mail-transmitting computer and its ingrown Internet. Go sit on your porch with a glass of vodka lemonade, a pad and pencil, and truly think.

To test my notion, plant me in a room with two hundred chaps at two hundred computers, give me a number two Ticonderoga pencil and a ten-cent Mohawk Red Indian pad, and I will outthink and outcreate the whole damn bunch.

Not Luddite ignorance against brightness this time but brightness against ignorance, against the easy fix, the lazy nonopinion, the naked emperor not seen without his clothes but the emperor's clothes empty of flesh, mind, and life.

A revolution, that is, against fireworks.

Some years back, addressing a virtual-reality congress of special affects—that word misspelled to illustrate people who *affect* to be bright but are simply the fuse lighters for sky explosions that blow off in winds to leave the sky empty—I cautioned them to get brain transplants.

Their creations having suffered triple bypasses away from the cerebrum to the groin or, perhaps worse, to sheer emptiness, I pleaded for true information, not false shows. They were serving Chinese dinners—you were hungry an hour later! No more vacuum-packed sound-bite histories. Not dodo sums but biographical analysis and philosophy.

Think! Do you really want to be in lightning-strike instant contact with every Nellie, Ned, and Noodge in the Universe? Do you wish e-mail by the bushel and ton or wish to send bags of boredom to friends innocently thinking they might get through the day without being struck senseless by your homespun gimcrack inspirations? Why not instead pierce two empty tin cans, insert thirty yards of twine, hold one can to your ear, give the other to a pal across the street so he can shout his revelations so loudly you don't need the can. Then do the reverse, as you did when you were a kid patrolling the neighborhood and waking neighbors with your yells.

Let William Faulkner be your guide. He was fired as postmaster in a southern town because he didn't want to be at the beck and call of any SOB with a two-cent stamp.

Pick up the phone. Give friends a chance *not* to answer. Use your car, go visit. But warn Aunt Nell and Cousin Billy Bob you're coming, so they can chugalug the gin.

Computer games? Family competitions to prove that everyone's brains were left behind in their mother? Why not prove that in a single night you can move from nursery to kinder-garten with aplomb?

Laptops as bedtime companions? Laptops cannot be cud-dled like a babe in your arms. Laptops cannot bed down with you midnights, along with Madame Bovary or Long John Silver or Hamlet's father's ghost. Pour salt on the laptop batteries and watch them sizzle like snails. Get a life.

Internet research? No! Step into a real library, swim in the aquarium of time, touch the books, open the books, smell the books, dog-ear the damned wondrous things with your canines. Wander the shadowed stacks, meet the Wizard and John Carter and Blind Pew coming the other way. Climb the stacks like an ape. Meet Verne on his way to the Moon, the first Sherpa on Everest, or Nemo. What's he doing up here at the bottom of the sea? Lug ten books home, with their scent of baking bread and their bright eyes and lively tongues. Then dash back to the bak-ery. The library, the library, the library.

Let's face it, there was only one place where my novel *Fahren-heit 451* could have been written: the basement typing room of the UCLA library, where, dashing up and downstairs with a bag-ful of dimes to feed the typewriter slot machines, I wallowed in the dim tides between stacks, sniffing in Tolstoy, breathing out Melville, then back downstairs to bang the Underwood.

Get a life!

Call your cat to help you kill that laptop mouse.

Glancing back at the twentieth century and promising that the twenty-first will be better, let's review some truths.

Since 1900, automobiles have truly hit ground, and lo! the highways fused sea to shining sea.

And with that invention, and the roads to cozen it, the slaves were freed. The cotton patches of the South were trampled by field hands in flight. The highways cried, "Quittin' time," and the pickers fled, slowly, and then with cheap cars and gas, in swarms, the word ELSEWHERE as bumper stickers.

The technologies of the twentieth century—radio, films, TV—sang psalms of far places, go find, go keep, and the Great Escape was on.

Without the invented car and its freedom gas, there would have been no exodus. Minus the sounds of distant occupations broadcast on crystal and heterodyne radios, the bust-out North, East, and West would have stillborn. Movie-house flickers showed what radios could not: far towns paved with gold, orange groves in which to hide the past, live for futures. Independence declared lay doggo until radio said, "Go! Get! Become!" Newsreels affirmed, and a promise of highways so fresh you left tire marks in tar. The pre–World War I trickle became the hallelujah midcentury scramble. Without the plane, train, and automobile, President Johnson would not have seen a dark sea of travelers mob the Mall and thus picked up his pen.

For the grumpers who say let's remake the twentieth century and do it right, let me list our virtues.

Dr. Salk's vaccine, which vanquished parents' dread when July arrived and children were in danger of being crippled or killed by polio.

Destroyed, en masse, all the other major diseases that decimated millions. Influenza, chickenpox, measles, scarlet fever, tuberculosis, gone. Almost forever. TB has returned but will be gone again.

In counterbalance? AIDS, syphilis, gonorrhea. But these will vanish by 2099.

Human beings will NOT, repeat NOT, be cloned in the new millennium. We already have been: twins. Who wants more?

All major American cities will be reconceived, rebuilt. We know *how* and will *do*.

State capitals could well relocate on Iroquois, Havasupai, and Algonquin casino reservations.

An Indian or Native American, your choice, will be president of the United States. Vice president will be a person of color whose ancestors stoked the Mississippi steamboats.

At long last, education will be arm-wrestled free of the Washington spoilers and pass into the creative hands of not yokels but locals.

As any half-bright student, mom, or "teach" knows, education is a hand-to-hand, in-your-face dialogue. Distant Washington elves and fairy horns do not drift downwind to waft over your typical schoolhouse; they are lost in static paper-snow blizzards. Education should not descend from the top but arise from the bottom. Its escalation will be given lift by inspired teachers, alert parents, and students who wander into classrooms bearing unfamiliar books, destined to be read at Canaveral, Moonbase, and New Chicago Mars. Quoting Admiral Byrd on his way to the South Pole: "Jules Verne leads me." H. G. Wells will sound-bite from computer harps that sing truths if you run a mouse over them. Arthur C. Clarke, Heinlein, Asimov, and others, born in space never to return, will teach nonreaders how and why to read. Their premise: Live forever. The suddenly-sit-upright student response: Yeah!

On a lesser level, consider that newborn vaudevillian: the videocassette. It will seize and dominate all future political campaigns. Realizing that the hourly bombardment of opinion is beyond funding, the various parties, right and left, will Mardi Gras a downslide of cassettes, light and dark, to flood our eyes and ears and tempt our blind paws to vote. The superb truth in dispersing videocassettes is that you trade your untruths with your neighbor and watch his window to see if it's played, then borrow *his* spin to cook your TV set and twitch your surfing finger. Thus, soon the donkey and elephant will clash midfield and sumo-wrestle across a minefield of sweaty miscalculations. These trumpet-and-bray tapes, distributed, will be el cheapo compared to cable or main-line time charges. Best of all, the outraged truths of vapid politicos can be saved for generations and rerun late nights to remind the sainted left and right that they are walking wounded. Hurling their crutches aside, they will try to protest their lies as living wits and be vote-tossed out the side exits.

And in the midst of this, with a confederation of astronautical nations and the unlimited Universe above, the Greatest War will occur. The Third World War, actually, a war against Space, Time, and Eternity, a war of creation rather than destruction, at the end of which some few will have suffered, others died, but most prevailed to inhabit the air and populate alien worlds.

With a space station built not in space but on the good gray foundation ground of the Moon, we will send celebratory fireworks to at last landfall Mars, not to photo-scan but landfall flesh-and-blood astronauts on the rim of that grand abyss, longer and wider than the U.S.A., and stare deep in its mirror to spy more futures.

In an essay published years ago, I described our destiny as "We are the Carpenters of an Unseen Cathedral," first seen with our intuition and then rocket-assembled in place. An architecture of belief in future life that speaks this motto:

Carpe diem, *seize the day*. But more: Witness and celebrate. We will ask ourselves why we were Earth-born in ignorance to lift our intelligence and outpace death. To what purpose?

An old question repeated like a celebratory prayer wheel.

Why mankind on Earth, faced with monkey-puzzle genetics? The answer is this:

The Universe needs to be seen. It cannot exist without us. If *we* vanish, the Cosmos vanishes.

Our ego speaks a superb lie to urge us to persist, to conquer time and its meltdown of flesh.

Our souls cry thanks to the Universe, the Cosmos, the God-head, for our birth and being. We need to prayerfully cry that thanks.

Space travel, then, is a thanksgiving journey with a Vatican Shinto Muslim Baptist choir to outpace Beethoven and shake the stars in their gyres.

We see, we know, we cry gratitudes and save the Universe from darkness by saving it with our sight, banking it in our souls, and speaking it in tongues. We do not go gentle into that good night, we go raving with joy and will settle for nothing less but reciprocal gratitude from the Cosmos, glad to be found and recognized.

Alexander Pope's *Rape of the Lock* puts it thus:

Now lakes of liquid gold, Elysian scenes,
And crystal domes and angels in machines.

And the angels, and devils, in machines will be us. On our way to doomsday, or headlong for heaven, and that heaven's name is Moon, Mars, and the Universe beyond, so small it nests in the human heart, so vast it explodes the human soul.

And by the end of the third millennium, what?

We will have footprinted the Moon, migrated to Mars, rico-cheted off Saturn's rings to reach out and touch a hoped-for world circumnavigating Alpha Centauri.

We will do just that to seed the Universe with bad and good, hope and despair, carrying the memory of Hitler and the promise of Christ.

We defy old Shakespeare's cry that we are just sound and fury signifying nothing. Our sounding fury will signify *something*. A silent Universe speaks because we speak. A blind Universe sees because we see. An unknowing Universe knows because we know.

Who says? I say.

So *you* will say it, and your children's children's children.

We will outlive war and shout-claim the Universe.

And live forever, or a million years. Whichever comes first.

THE RABBIT HOLE LOST AND FOUND BOOK SHOPPE (UNDATED)

As you walk, behold!

In the pavement below . . .

A rather largish Rabbit Hole.

We are, in fact, standing on the hole.

It is, in further fact, a hole with a transparent crystal lid upon it so that we can seemingly stand upon mere nothingness, simple air, and look down at:

Alice falling down the long hole.

The White Rabbit falling down the deep shaft.

Huck Finn and Tom Sawyer, holding candles, falling after . . .

Long John Silver falling, cursing.

Nemo's *Nautilus* falling, sailing.

Ahab pursuing his White Whale, falling after the whole blasted mob.

Black Beauty running, falling down, down . . .

The Cyclops, falling . . .

The Medusa, falling, along with Helen of Troy, Romeo and Juliet . . . The Hunchback of Notre Dame! Hamlet! Othello!

And, pursuing the lot, a fleet of starships, rockets, interplanetary craft, flashing, firing down, down away.

And as we look down at this vast hole that we stand upon and watch the waterfall, the cascade of famous characters, we hear them name themselves, so we can identify the person or persons thus tossed down the literary mine shaft:

"Huck . . . Huck Finn . . . Tom . . . Tom Sawyer . . . Quasi-modo . . . Romeo . . . Long John Silver . . . Rebecca of Sunnybrook—"

And we look up at the sign over the bright storefront that, not surprisingly, reads:

THE RABBIT HOLE LOST AND FOUND BOOK SHOPPE!

Our eye is further drawn on our right to view:

In his own window arcade display:

Edgar Allan Poe, an audioanimatronic life-size figure, with pale full-moon brow, sad mustache, seated with pen and ink and parchment paper.

Upon his shoulder sits the Raven, dictating:

And as the Raven dictates lines from various Poe stories, from the top of Poe's head in a cloud of nocturnal steams and fog brewings, a misting of phantom shapes, ghosts, cats, witches, beasts, monsters drawn and etched by our old Spanish friend Goya. These nightmares fly up and away into the night winds above Poe's head, monster after monster, beast after beast . . . some from Goya's black-period paintings.

So we combine literature and drawing/etching/painting.

Finally, as we watch, the Raven quotes the ending of "The Fall of the House of Usher," and all, all of the images, mixed with masonry, towers, windows, doors, the whole architecture of miserable doom sinks down into the dark tarn within Poe's head.

The Raven shuts up. Great sounds of cataclysm. Great surges of water. Poe shuts his eyes. His hand stops moving. He rests.

Thus riven, we turn our eyes to our left.

On the opposite side of the entrance, we find another, greater display, a window filled with galaxies of stars toward which, in which, fly fleets of rockets, starships, away and away, mixed perhaps with floating, flying, sinking book covers of the authors the mighty ships represent.

So we have three visual enticements, each of a size imaginatively large or large within smallness: Rabbit Hole, Poe, and View of the Entire Galactic Empire, what is there for us to do but . . . raise the crystal lid and . . .

Rush down and slide to a halt in the Rabbit Hole Lost and Found Book Shoppe!

Where we find intermixed with soaring shelves, spiral staircases, and walls with mysterious poke holes in them:

Embedded in the floor here and there all through the future-world book shoppe, a series of further crystal-lidded Rabbit Holes. For instance:

In the middle of a Younger Children's Section, an uproar, uppour of beasts, dragons, chimeras, monsters would fall out of a bright/dark sky to strike against our soles, vanish, to be replaced by more beasts falling toward us out of a sky beneath our feet.

In the Aviation Section, a Rabbit Hole sky in which a parade of all the grandest aircraft from the Wright Brothers on up to our shuttle into space would parade by, endlessly.

In the Archaeology Section, we would peer directly down into Tutankhamen's tomb with all its glorious junk-room display of gold, turquoise, and lapis lazuli.

Nearby would stand a replica, above the surface of the floor, above the hole, of the Tutankhamen mummy with its incredible golden mask. The lips of the mask would move from time to time, and we would hear it whisper if we bent near:

Would you know the ages? Would you know the tomb? Would you dig bones? Find mummies? Seek the past? Climb the pyramids? Be lost in the dead valley of the kings? Here lie Egyptian bones in Egyptian tombs with Egyptian curses. Find it. Know it. Put your hand to the shelf. Winnow the bones. Choose among mummies. Read the books . . . !

And, of course, on either side of the mummy case are displayed books on archaeology and, along the top of the shelf, a small replica of the golden Sphinx.

Moving on into the Science-Fiction Section, we would find various robots by various shelves, each capable of speech when touched, to describe books, events in books, grand cataclysms, births of suns and moons, deaths of stars. These robots stand guard over yet another Rabbit Hole in which spaceships and armadas fight titanic wars or strange beasts parade into a strange star-bound ark, two by two, all colors, all sizes, from all kinds of far planets.

Interspersed through the bookstore would be spiral staircases, some of them leading up into cliffs of stacks about . . . er . . . mountains, so you do indeed climb that spiral of steps to reach a lofty perch to get your alpine books . . . or . . . conversely . . . the spiral steps go down, down into the floor to a special subterranean room full of books on . . . of course . . . the sea!

The spiral staircases going *up* would have, embedded in a corkscrew crystal shield glass, painted pictures of mountain climbs that would spin upward as the images in a barber pole spin up, so that readers would be visually induced to climb *up* with the moving-upward gliding climbers.

The staircases going *down* would have images of sea divers going down, spiraling down, so, conversely, our readers would be drawn down into the room below the book shoppe's floor.

At the main entrance of the shoppe would be a computer robot that, spoken to, or touched/typed for data, would supply said information either by voice or by printout . . . TYPE IN YOUR NEEDS and the robot would instruct you to go past THE RED STACKS, THE YELLOW STACKS, and to BLUE STACK, SHELF 3 or SHELF 4. Also printed out would be additional information on similar books at your local library, plus recordings/tapes/films of same.

Interspersed throughout our book shoppe, similar computers either as silver and gold futuristic robots or shapes like King Tut or inside ancient sea divers' helmets, would answer our questions, give us directions.

Here and there throughout the shoppe would be conveniently placed window seats where readers can sit or curl up with books and look out upon green rolling Irish hills or Sahara dunes or the lamasery in Tibet, or look upon Oz itself with its roads leading off to four different-colored countries, or upon the Mad King Ludwig's castle or on Spanish pirate sea coves where corsair ships are putting in. There should be at least eight such windows where readers can pause, sit, rest, and read awhile.

On display as we move we find:

The Michelangelo inkwell in which a twenty-inch-tall wax figurine Boy David is suspended in a light blue ink so we can look through the transparent sides of the inkwell and see the small figure there, surrounded by calibrated walls. At the touch of a button, we can lower the ink, even as Michelangelo did. At the instant of our doing so, a thirty-foot-tall oblong of marble standing nearby shrapnels itself away under the blows of an invisible chisel and hammer. With concussions of sound, we watch the gigantic Boy David broken out of his stone prison, revealed inch by inch as the ink is lowered in the inkwell so we can measure small against large and prove a history of Michelangelo's birthing David at a touch of our hand.

And then again:

Either inside the shoppe in an alcove or outside as a monolithic display, we should construct a gigantic light/electric sketch board whose translucent surface would be lit by a thousand small, embedded lights in primary colors of red/blue/yellow, mixtures of which would give us our purples, greens, and oranges . . . super Georges Seurat! A person standing at a small computer sketch pad below, utilizing a stylus, could draw a quick sketch instantly reproduced on the large image screen. The sketch would be photographed instantly, and the "artist" would have a permanent record of his or her large "masterpiece" created by light. Depending on the ability of the individual artists, of course, we would have some highly original or awful light works on display during an electric encounter.

Throughout the book shoppe, in various walls, would be literary poke holes . . . holes where children or adults could stick their heads into darkness.

As soon as a person stuck his or her head into such a pokehole place, his head would intercept an invisible light beam, causing a film to run or a small audioanimatronic figurine to shout up at him.

In one poke hole, Captain Bligh down below in his boat would cry, "I'll be back, Mr. Christian, to make you pay!"

In another, Cathy would stand in a snowstorm crying, "Heathcliff . . . oh, Heathcliff!"

In yet another, once you got your head in, you would see all about, below, a Parisian mob, with Madame Defarge knitting, looking up at you. A quiet voice would say, "It is a far, far better thing that I do, than I have ever done. . . ." And *CHOMP*. The sound of a guillotine sliding down, with a gentle touch on the back of your neck . . . !

Another poke hole and you see, laid out before you: a pit, a young man, and a . . . descending . . . *pendulum*!

Or . . . Huck and Tom gliding by on a river on a raft, calling up, "Hey, come on, water's fine . . . fishing's fancy fine!"

BEYOND 1984 (1979)

Don't look now, but the eighties are almost upon us. Which means that the usual Chicken Little end-of-the-world doomsters are rushing in circles, colliding with themselves and shouting, "Head for the hills, the dam is broke!" Here comes 1984. Watch out, there's Big Brother.

Bulrushes and sauerkraut.

Nineteen eighty-four will show up, but not as a Kremlin gargoyle or an Orwellian beast. We have, for the time being anyway, knocked Big Brother into the next century. With luck, and if we keep our eye on the ballot box and our chameleon politicos, he may never recover. Meanwhile, just beyond 1984, a truly grand year awaits us. Nineteen eighty-six will be a special time. Why special and why grand? If 1984 once symbolized the worst of man, 1986 might just possibly symbolize nothing but the best. For that is the year we earthlings will enjoy a close encounter of the fourth kind.

A visitor from beyond will park itself on our solar doorstep for some few months, then vanish like some Christmas ghost. We will not see it again for another seventy-six years. How shall we react? In one scenario we will toss ourselves high in celebrations to meet this ghost. We will stand forth in space and wave the cold beast in. We will laugh in its face. We will probe its icy flesh and swirl our technological matador's cape as it rushes by us at some hundred thousand miles per hour. We will pierce its heart with the finest, brightest swords that science can forge, then offer to crowds around the world the secret of the birth of the solar system.

In another scenario we will watch an artist's conception of the event on television, our faces illuminated by the pale light of the tube. A commentator will mourn, "Maybe next time."

The visitor, of course, is Halley's comet. The villain is Congress, which must approve the funds for this grand scheme. And who are the people who would play tag with the cosmic train? The amiable "mad" scientists at the Jet Propulsion Laboratory in Pasadena, California.

Those are the same wild folks who helped bring you Mars Viking landings I and II. The folks who remind me of the old Bob Hope–Jerry Colonna routine in which Hope shouts at the sky, "Colonna, what are you doing up there?"

"Building a bridge—starting at the top."

"But," cries Hope, "you can't do that!"

Colonna shrugs and turns to his workers. "All right, boys, tear it down."

But the blueprinters at JPL won't tear anything down. They are used to building imaginary bridges, starting at the top, then riveting a foundation under the dream before it blows away.

Those are the folks who want to build a bridge to Mars, who would send a probe there that would return with samples from the surface. Those are the folks who want to build a bridge to Titan to sample the atmosphere of Saturn's most literary moon. They would orbit Jupiter, land on Mercury, and send a robot to summer camp on Mars. They are dreamers who, when they awake, try to sell their dreams to NASA and a skinflint Congress.

If Congress wants to share the dream of a Halley's-comet encounter, it will have to reach into its purse and pull out some $500 million. And it will have to do so in the near future. If it waits too long, there won't be time for the experimental draftings, the many test failures, and the final successes that plague and reward such grandiose exercises. The bureaucracy that made Big Brother possible will kill the dream.

One plan to rendezvous with Halley's comet has already bitten the dust. In 1977, scientists at JPL were toying with the idea of a solar sail, a giant kite, a stringless wonder, with all our souls as its endless tail. The sail was to be powered by the light of the sun.

Pure sunlight can do that? It can. Light rays exert pressure in the form of protons—massless particles. When these particles strike a surface, they are, in effect, a supersonic wind blowing against a sail.

The original comet-intercept plan was simple and elegant. The sail would be a thin breath of Mylar plastic skinned out over some aluminum spider that might well measure as much as half a mile wide. This vast experiment would be tucked in special shuttles and launched into space. There astronauts would scramble to unfurl the beauty, raise the sail, finish out the kite, then hop back into the shuttles and let the sun push the sail with its massless winds. Set free, the sail would be controlled and balanced by vanes.

Slowly it would build speed, until it reached the hundred thousand miles per hour necessary to make the rendezvous. Unlike normal rockets, which are limited in the amount of fuel they can carry and in their final speed, the solar sail would find its fuel in space.

To reach rendezvous speed, a launch would have to have

been made by 1981. The seed money should have been granted in 1978. It didn't happen. NASA looked at the comet-intercept project, compared the benefits with other priority projects (including another comet project), and crossed off the solar sail from its 1978 shopping list.

The scientists at JPL were undaunted. They had an alternative propulsion system on the drawing boards: the ion drive, a galactic butterfly that can spin sunlight into electricity, to emit a soft violet blast. Like the solar sail, it finds its fuel in space. Dr. Ken Atkins, head of the comet-intercept program at JPL, pulled the ion drive out of the hat and said, "Lo, we can't build up speed to rendezvous, but we can cut across the path of the visitor and drop an instrument package down the throat of the comet."

And just for a touch of class, the JPL plan offered a two-for-one shot: The ion-drive craft could fly by Halley's comet and then, two years later, rendezvous with Tempel 2, a bright little visitor that drops by every 5.3 years. We could pace the comet past Mercury without setting ourselves aflame, then tag along when it moved back out to hide itself in the mine-shaft universe.

The project can be done; the only question is, will it be done?

That depends on the president and/or the Congress. The latter is questionable. Space is low down on their priority scale.

Why *should* we spend half a billion dollars on a comet? Because we must confront the mystery. What *is* a comet? The question runs back beyond Bethlehem, before the birth of the pharaohs.

Is a comet a somewhat soiled but mighty snowball hurled from the left hand of God some winter morning He has long since forgotten? Is it the breath of some old sun now dead but whose final sigh still comes to whisper 'round our yard? Is it a halation of dusts and interplanetary cinders, fragments of meteoroid flaked from some chance encounter with a far planetary system?

The commonest theory, advanced by Fred Whipple in 1950, describes cometary bodies as blizzards of frozen gases and nonvolatile solids. Small comets are a few hundred meters in diameter. The largest measure twenty miles across. As a comet enters the solar system, the sun heats the frozen sphere. The solar wind blows the debris into a tail a million miles in length.

The scientific community is very interested in the Comet Rendezvous Program. It is likely that the debris caught in the frozen grasp of the comet head is primordial. As old as the universe. The Halley probe could analyze the dust by spectrometer and magnetometer. Cameras could give us a view of the birth scars of the solar system. It is an opportunity too important to pass up because of mere economics.

Of course, there are other comets. The boys at JPL have come up with several alternative missions between now and the turn of the century. But Halley's comet is so American. Indeed, when I first heard of the project, I suggested calling the probe the *Mark Twain*. Why?

Well, now, Mark Twain was born in 1835, when Halley's comet tore across the sky to welcome him. Doubtful of miracles, suspicious of heaven, nonetheless Twain later predicted he would depart this Earth when the comet came back to fetch him. It did, and Twain did, in 1910.

Halley's comet has a power over men's imaginations that far exceeds shuttle diplomacy or the best of prime-time television.

At the core of our *Mark Twain* celestial explorer would be cameras and multipurpose devices to photograph the comet, take its temperature, and, with luck, knife through to its bright interior. The instrument package we would hurl into the face of Halley's comet is doomed—at fifty-seven kilometers per second, the comet devours everything in its path. Another fate awaits the surviving part of the ion-drive craft. It will head out beyond the orbit of Mars, turn tail, and play catch-up with Tempel 2 in 1988. The two will head together for the sun—and for six months we will listen in on their conversation. The ion-drive craft may be captured by the comet, or it may wander off onto a solo journey. It depends on the courtship of gravity.

Then again, perhaps we can hurl these robot devices in such a way as to track the Tempel 2 comet on its entire circumnavigation of our solar system. Playing dead for a good part of the journey, our sensing machines could be programmed to reactivate in what might be called Project Lazarus. In the far mortuary reaches of space, we could call them awake so as to test the vision of Jupiter's giant red eye or shake the frost from Pluto's back porch.

Think, then, when these long-distance runners return to speak in tongues late in the twenty-first century to tell us of far attic places where we as living flesh cannot follow. Someday, yes, our flesh will landfall Pluto and beyond. But for now our riddle-solving electric children must roam the vast star meadows to graph the heartbeat of Halley's cosmic beast.

What's holding up this grand cosmic parade?

As in the past, cash in the box.

With a military budget sucking $129 billion away from cities, away from schools, away from hospitals, that inevitably means away from space, time, comets, and our possible future survival.

Plus, we have been in a down cycle from overexposure to moon landings, astronauts, and the thousands of hours TV networks poured on us, ladling out multitudinous facts but little

insight. We have had our feet and minds, as I have often ob-
served, encased in Cronkite. Without poets, philosophers, or
even smart political observers such as Eric Sevareid, the cosmic
question goes a-begging year on year.

Meanwhile, because we are so busy building arms to sell to
Arabs to scare the Israelis and selling yet further arms to scared
Jews to rescare Saudi Arabia and friends, we have no time to
stand and stare. We opt out of being philosophers. To think
would seem to be the worst thing we might accuse ourselves
of. To think *imaginatively* is beyond comment. Dreamers, we
snort, stand aside! Reality is the only tonic. Facts are the only
medicine. Yet we are full of facts; we burst with data and are
not made well. Our spirit flags on the pole.

Can Halley's comet play doctor to our souls? Can the ion-
drive craft we build lift our blood and make us truly care about
not just mere existence now but futures yet unplumbed?

Why bother? a voice cries from the balcony. Who cares?
What's all the fuss and star feathers about?

Very simply: We march back to Olympus.

How's that again?

Well, now, we Earth people are great ones, aren't we, for
picking ourselves up by the scruff and heaving ourselves out of
the Garden or off the holy mount? We shake ourselves together some facts and add them up to doom, don't we?

Consider: Two thousand years ago, everything was all right
with man's universe. We inhabited a planet around which the
sun moved as if we were central to its existence. The stars did
the same. We were God's navel, and everyone found us good to
look upon.

Then along came various theologians and astronomers, and
next thing we know, we're evicted, both from Eden and from
Mount Olympus. We found ourselves out in the rain with a

bunch of demoted Apollos, Aphrodites, Zeuses, and Titans. It would take a few thousand years before we got around to naming some rockets for the lost gods.

Meanwhile, the astronomers told us that we were not central to anything. We were, in fact, inhabitants of a rather smallish rabbit pellet whirling about a minor sun in the subbasement of a galaxy that did not much care whether we came or went, lived or died, suffered or survived.

The knock on the head that this seeming fact gave us unsettled our egos for quite a few hundred years.

If Copernicus and Galileo and Kepler told us these things, they must be right. If Darwin added that we were merely a bright chimpanzee wheeling a Maserati or a Pinto along time's highway, well, then, why bother to get out of bed in the morning?

But we have got out of bed, and we have gone to the Moon, and then we have reached up and fingerprinted Mars. And to those who look at data and say, Mars is empty, there is no life there, we shout:

There *is* life on Mars, and it is *us*.

We move into the universe. We name ourselves, along with our rockets, after old deities. We make ourselves central to existence, knowing not how far we must travel before we meet other mirrors of God staring back into His vast gaze.

For, you see, while facts are important, interpretation of facts is the final builder or destroyer of man and his dream. If we choose to find ourselves minor, or of no worth, the dust will burn and hide our bones. But if we choose to step back into the Garden, devour the apple, throw the snake out into the ditch, and survive forever out beyond the Coalsack Nebula, the choice is ours. We will build Olympus and put on our crowns once more.

That is what our encounter with Halley's comet is all about.

So there you have it: 1986 coming on fast. Here comes our chance to reach up. We would gently touch the passing face of that cold creature, the looming features of that strange matter and force on its blind way 'round the cosmos. We would do so with that puzzled, infinite curiosity that is the beginning of love.

Do we miss this chance? Do we let time and space churn by without hastening to leap aboard? Do we keep our giant man-made pterodactyl home and lock our best dreams with it, in a box?

I think not. For some century soon, we will be falling out there ourselves. Our dear flesh will outpace that lovely comet.

Meanwhile, our fabulous machines must go for us, do for us, and come back smoking a pipe filled with incredible data, to tamp Mark Twain observations in our ears to lean us toward survival.

If our mind flies now, our machines fly later, and our souls fly to follow both in twenty-first-century salvation armies of space. And the higher we fly, the more 1984 will recede like a failed threat, an evil promise disconnected, a hell boarded over, a death done in and buried by life.

We will write a better book then. Its title will be *1986*, and its hero will be the Great White Comet, and Huck Finn's father's kite will lay itself out on the solar winds to welcome it.

As for the comet, it will arrive like doom.

But it will go back out around with annunciations.

What will it announce?

Ourselves, of course, birthing ourselves back into the lap of God.

Telling Him that soon, soon, oh, very soon, we will drop in for a visit. . . .

And *stay* for 10 billion years.

THE ARDENT BLASPHEMERS (1962)

Consider America, first of all the new breed of nations.

Consider America, a nation, because of its newness, ardent in its blasphemy.

Set in motion by the centrifuge of the great wheel of the industrial revolution, this people flung themselves across sea prairies to stand on New England rimrock and fling themselves yet on across land prairies. Shocking other ages, they blasphemed down the meadows and over hills as ancient as the memory of Jerusalem.

Consider America, her fire-dragon locomotives huffing out vast devil bursts of fluming spark, setting the lion grass afire as they went.

Come to a forest, cut it down. Come to a mountain, quarry it to pebbles. Skip the pebbles across God's lakes. Build *new* mountains, finally, upright, and ornamented with man's prideful encrustations. Then run men up and down elevator shafts to a heaven no longer believed in from a hell much better ignored.

Consider the authors who lived in and with these men and wrote to channel this blasphemy, express it in symbols about which such men could enthuse like devil children. With a new nation being dreamed to life, set to rights with fabulous new toys, the uneasy dreamers cast about and came up with two most ardent blasphemers:

Herman Melville.

Jules Verne.

"American" authors, both.

Melville, the New Englander, and Verne, the Frenchman, you say, Americans both?

"American," yes, in their newness and their attack upon the universe and this world rolling through that universe.

Another nation could have been "American" first. The seeds of man's mechanical reaction to nature were cast forth first in England and France. But the flowering of what other ages might have considered an insidious tree was in this raw nation under God that which would soon ask Him to move over, jump aside, step down. We might not even ask His pardon while we scourged the mineral gut, packed once-holy echoes in electronic boxes to deal them forth commercially, split atoms as handily as peas, and dared God to answer back in equal thunders.

I say another nation could have done this. But the accidents of time and circumstance dubbed us unholy first. Others follow us in our sacrilege: the Japanese and his insect-clicking camera, the Frenchman flung about by our LP jive, the Italian hopping Rome's hills on angry adaptations of our motorbikes.

The sacrilege was inevitable.

The wheel invented by some fine fool of a first blasphemer, once set in motion just beyond old Egypt, rolls up in the late eighties of our time such dust clouds as would dim the bright visage of any spoiled God. Wheels within wheels within wheels rolled forth upon our land and, later, way in the middle of our outraged God's air.

And being firstest with the mostest, we not only *did* but *read* and, having read, did *more*.

And Jules Verne was our text and testament, followed close by packs of "evil" boys like Tom Swift and his Flying Machine plus his A.C.-D.C I.B.M. Power-Circuited Grandmother.

I Sing the Body Electric! cried Whitman.

And Americans wound tight their robot devices and set them free to gnaw ugliness across the territories that now, very late, we must clean up after.

But let us go back to our literary beginnings.

Why, in introducing you to this book by Jules Verne, do I summon forth the lunar name of Herman Melville? What relation do I see between a Frenchman benevolent as a good uncle in his eccentricities and strange Cousin Herman, who some thought best kept in America's attic?

From the viewpoint of Gothic times peering ahead at the tidal wave of the future, let me set up these two men.

God, after all, was in His heaven a long while, and things went well for Him, if not His children, upon earth. Those born-but-to-die inhabited His churches, and if they questioned, questions were best kept mum in one's mouth or like gum behind the ear.

But send these God-doting children free from Europe, strew and scrabble them across a whole continental surprise, hand them commotions and contraptions of steam and whiffling iron, and they pant up frenzies of revenge against God for having maltreated them down the eons.

Out of questions suddenly posed and needs suddenly found most needful, as the steam blew off and the proud dust settled, we found:

Mad Captain Ahab.

Mad Captain Nemo.

Moby Dick, the great White Whale.

Nautilus, the whale-seeming submarine, first of its hidden and terrific sort, soaring through sea meadows among sinner sharks and true leviathans.

Look how these two "evil" men implement their "blasphemy."

"Call me Ishmael."

So Melville strikes forth on his search for Moby Dick. In his first chapter we find:

> . . . Why upon your first voyage as a passenger, did you yourself feel such a mystical vibration, when first told that you and your ship were now out of sight of land? Why did the old Persians hold the sea holy? Why did the Greeks give it a separate deity, and own brother of Jove? Surely all this is not without meaning. And still deeper the meaning of that story of Narcissus, who because he could not grasp the tormenting, mild image he saw in the fountain, plunged into it and was drowned. But that same image, we ourselves see in all rivers and oceans. It is the image of the ungraspable phantom of life; and this is the key to it all.

Why does Ishmael go to sea?

> Chief among these motives was the overwhelming idea of the great whale himself. Such a portentous and mysterious monster roused all my curiosity. Then the wild and distant seas where he rolled his island bulk; the undeliverable, nameless perils of the whale; these, with all the attending marvels of a thousand Patagonian sights and sounds, helped to sway me to my wish. . . .
>
> By reason of these things, then, the whaling voyage was welcome; the great flood-gates of the wonder-world swung open, and in the wild conceits that swayed me to my purpose, two and two there floated into my inmost soul, endless processions of the whale, and mid most of them all, one grand hooded phantom, like a snow hill in the air.

In *20,000 Leagues Under the Sea*, Jules Verne starts thus:

> The year 1866 was marked by a strange event, an un-
> explainable occurrence which is undoubtedly still fresh
> in everyone's memory. . . . Several ships had recently met
> at sea "an enormous thing," a long slender object which
> was sometimes phosphorescent and which was infinitely
> larger and faster than a whale.

Verne continues:

> The facts concerning this apparition . . . agreed closely
> with one another as to the structure of the object or crea-
> ture in question, the incredible speed of its movements,
> the surprising power of its locomotion and the strange
> life with which it seemed endowed. If it was a member of
> the whale family, it was larger than any so far classified by
> scientists. . . .
> But it did exist—there was no denying this fact any
> longer—and considering the natural inclination of the
> human brain toward objects of wonder, one can under-
> stand the excitement produced throughout the world by
> this supernatural apparition. . . .

So two books begin. Both set somewhat the same tone, both
strike chords that might recur within the framework of the
book to follow. Yet swiftly we perceive rank differences. We
soon know that while Uncle Jules is mostly gently mad, Cousin
Herman is beyond the pale.

We set sail with Ishmael, who, unknowing, is in the clutches
of wild Ahab, seeking some universal truth shaped to a monster
all frightful white named Moby Dick.

We set sail almost simultaneously with Professor Aronnax and Ned Land and Conseil on the *Abraham Lincoln* in search of this other mystery that

> in every big city . . . became the fashion: it was sung in cafés, derided in newspapers and discussed on the stage. Scandal sheets had a marvelous opportunity to print all kinds of wild stories. Even ordinary newspapers—always short of copy—printed articles about every huge, imaginary monster one could think of, from the white whale, the terrible "Moby Dick" of the far north, to the legendary Norse kraken. . . .

So we suspect that Uncle Jules has touched minds somewhere down the line with Cousin Herman.

But without any real exchange or superblending of madness.

Mr. Verne will go his own way with his "educated" vengeance, leaving Melville with his Shakespearean terrors and laments.

We do not meet Moby Dick face-to-face; we have only Ahab's leg torn off in retrospect, until very late in Melville.

But Verne, in chapter VI of *20,000 Leagues*, heaves his "monster" to view and swallows our Jonahs whole and entire.

Thus ending the tale as Melville might end it?

No, thus starting to show us the vast differences between the odd American-type French writer and the truly driven New England author/sailor soon to be despairing customs inspector.

Let us compare some few quotes from each writer.

Here are some from *Moby Dick:*

> His three boats stove around him, and oars and men both whirling in the eddies; one captain, seizing the line-

knife from his broken prow, had dashed at the whale. . . .
That captain was Ahab. And then it was, that suddenly
sweeping his sickle-shaped lower jaw beneath him, Moby
Dick had reaped away Ahab's leg, as a mower a blade of
grass in the field. No turbaned Turk, no hired Venetian or
Malay, could have smote him with more seeming
malice. . . . Ever since that almost fatal encounter, Ahab
had cherished a wild vindictiveness against the whale, all
the more fell for that in his frantic morbidness he at last
came to identify with him, not only all his bodily woes,
but all his intellectual and spiritual exasperations. The
White Whale swam before him as the monomaniac in-
carnation of all those malicious agencies which some
deep men feel eating in them, till they are left living on
with half a heart and half a lung. . . . All that most maddens and torments; all that stirs up the lees of things; all
truth with malice in it; all that cracks the sinews and
cakes the brain; all the subtle demonisms of life and
thought; all evil, to crazy Ahab, were visibly personified,
and made practically assailable in Moby Dick. He piled
upon the whale's white hump the sum of all the general
rage and hate felt by his whole race from Adam down;
and then, as if his chest had been a mortar, he burst his
hot heart's shell upon it.

Also, Ahab, speaking to Starbuck:

Hark ye yet again,—the little lower layer. All visible
objects, man, are but as pasteboard masks. But in each
event—in the living act, the undoubted deed—there,
some unknown but still reasoning thing puts forth the
mouldings of its features from behind the unreasoning

mask. If man will strike, strike through the mask! How can the prisoner reach outside except by thrusting through the wall? To me, the white whale is that wall, shoved near to me. Sometimes I think there's naught beyond. But 'tis enough. He tasks me; he heaps me; I see in him outrageous strength, with an inscrutable malice sinewing it. That inscrutable thing is chiefly what I hate; and be the white whale agent, or be the white whale principal, I will wreak that hate upon him. Talk not to me of blasphemy, man: I'd strike the sun if it insulted me.

Compare the above with these quotes from Verne's somewhat more differently "touched" Nemo:

Professor . . . I'm not what you would call a civilized man! I've broken with all society for reasons which I alone can appreciate. I therefore don't obey its rules, and I advise you never to refer to them again in front of me!

Aronnax asks Nemo:

"You love the sea, don't you, Captain?"
"Yes, I love it! The sea is everything. It covers seven-tenths of the globe. Its breath is pure and healthy. It is an immense desert where a man is never alone, for he can feel life quivering all about him. The sea is only a receptacle for all the prodigious, supernatural things that exist inside it; it is only movement and love; it is the living infinite, as one of your poets has said. And in fact, Professor, it contains the three kingdoms of nature—mineral, vegetable, and animal. This last is well represented by the four groups of zoophytes, by the three classes of articu-

lata, by the five classes of mollusks, by the three classes of vertebrates, mammals and reptiles, and by those innumerable legions of fish, that infinite order of animals which includes more than thirteen thousand species, only one-tenth of which live in fresh water. The sea is a vast reservoir of nature. The world, so to speak, began with the sea, and who knows but that it will also end in the sea! There lies supreme tranquillity. The sea does not belong to tyrants. On its surface, they can still exercise their iniquitous rights, fighting, destroying one another and indulging in their other earthly horrors. But thirty feet below its surface their power ceases, their influence dies out and their domination disappears! Ah, Monsieur, one must live—live within the ocean! Only there can one be independent! Only there do I have no masters! There I am free!"

How different from Melville's:

When beholding the tranquil beauty and brilliancy of the ocean's skin, one forgets the tiger heart that pants beneath it; and would not willingly remember, that this velvet paw but conceals a remorseless fang.

And, in a tranquil, golden moment, Starbuck muses:

Loveliness unfathomable, as ever lover saw in his young bride's eye!—Tell me not of thy teeth-tiered sharks, and thy kidnapping cannibal ways. Let faith oust fact; let fancy oust memory; I look deep down and do believe.

But Ahab will have none of it. He rejects what Nemo gladly accepts.

The sea, with all its terror fleshed in beauty, is preferred by Nemo. Here ignorant hunters hunt from hunger. Above, intelligent men, sated at feasts, hunt from needs best not thought on save in nightmares of sadism and wanton destruction. To kill with the teeth is one thing. To kill with the hand, connected to the heart and thinking brain, is quite another.

"Strike through the mask!" cries Ahab.

Better than that, Nemo might reply in an imaginary rebuttal, I will *build* behind the mask, I will *inhabit* the white whale.

After a shocked silence, Nemo might continue something like this:

I will create me a symbol of the deep, a manifestation of God's huge wonders, submersible, long-ranging, capably destructive, submissive to my commands, and I will course ocean seas in same, to spread a more personal and therefore more constructive terror in the world. I will not run after Moby Dick. I will rear him whole and entire and live in his belly and be the Mystery, myself.

So, in sum, Nemo skins together and rivets tight the very symbol most feared and whispered of by Ahab's mind and Ahab's crew. Casting aside any doubts, precluding any inhibitions, Nemo intrudes to the monster's marrow, disinhabits mysticism, evicts terrors like so much trash, and proceeds to police the universe beneath, setting it to rights, harvesting its strange crops, be they animal, vegetable, or mineral—gold from sunken fool's ships to be distributed to the world's needy.

In this we find then that Verne is less blasphemous than Melville. He does not so much try to find and kill God in His lounging room as set His miraculous kitchen to percolating in synchronous, perceivable, and therefore serenity-inducing rhythms. Given choices, Melville's Ahab would blow up the clock tower. Verne's Nemo would collect the exploded parts, put the whole back better than new, and ask the world's citizens to tell their lives by it, be on time for one another from now on.

Verne accepts the natural world and would ask all men to accept its secret ways and join in making themselves over nearer to the hidden heart of this secret so as to utilize it, channel it, reconstruct it where necessary, to give man extra years and vitality.

Melville cannot accept and with Ahab rages at the blind maunderings of a God he cannot comprehend.

Ah, well, says Verne, let us work, let us think, then let us work again until we sweat. We shall win through, or die trying.

No, says Melville, we cannot win. And vainly thrusts the harpoon to deflate the God-symboled Whale.

Verne cares less about killing the symbol, more of rendering the Leviathan out for oil to light the flickerful lamps of a thinking world.

Thinking maddens Ahab.

Thinking only half maddens Nemo, more often enlivens and solves problems for him and others who inhabit Verne's literary worlds.

Ahab is mad at the God universe.

Nemo, more practically, is mad at man himself for not using his gift of brains.

Ahab, being irrationally disturbed at the Invisible, can do little.

Nemo, being distressed at God's children, has at least somewhere to start, material to work with, evil and good men to choose among, dirt to be swept out of corners and from under rugs.

Ahab, in trying to search everywhere, finds nothing.

Nemo, content with good beginnings, looks no further than the next man and scans his face to guess his dream, and if the dream be bad, there is always the ocean depth to live in, gathering yet richer harvests whereby to relieve the oppressed.

So in the long journey through *Moby Dick*, we follow Ahab, knighted by the whale who did so by tearing him asunder, and wearing his terrible crown of now self-inflicted thorns, self-appointing himself to a tragic end.

We wonder what Nemo would have thought of all this?

Glancing in from the kitchen, where he might be busy serving forth foods to button up men's souls and sluice their veins with revivifying wonder, Nemo might well debate who that demented sea king was, unnecessarily throwing and dragging himself about the throne room. We could well imagine Nemo hurrying in to offer a bracing hot drink or finally slapping Ahab once across the face, seizing his shoulders to shake him, at last, and tell him to behave.

Faced with similar cataclysms, Ahab, we know, would go down with his ship, shaking his fists at fate.

While Nemo would vanish beneath the sea still bailing out water with his cupped hands.

Ahab's ship pursues an unpursuable God, crying out against His characteristically ill behavior.

Nemo's ship pursues men to remind them of their wickedness, to improve it or be sunk.

Ahab's ship moves most of the time in nightmare.

Nemo's moves in kaleidoscopic wonders, in rainbow beauties of life thrown forth in multitudinous displays. Only man is nightmare, and Nemo has a better dream to give him as anodyne.

Moby Dick rams Ahab's *Pequod* because the ship is the engine of blasphemy, directed at the Mystery.

Nemo's *Nautilus* rams naval ships because they blaspheme against the better and best spirit of humankind.

In the long history of the world, God's motto was writ on man's brow this way:

Yours not to reason why.
Yours to be born and die.

So Melville's Whale resents inquiry.

But Verne's *Nautilus* is the machine of curiosity, erasing the above motto, prolonging a searchful blasphemy into construction and jigsawing the grand puzzle into a whole.

Ahab orders God to re-form Himself in a better image.

Nemo asks mankind to re-form in cleaner, higher-spirited, well-mannered ranks.

Both men, being reformers, inevitably destroy for their purposes.

Ahab takes all with him to the sea bottom in his Shakespearean frenzy.

Nemo, less mad, like many reformers nevertheless winds up killing men to make them behave. Death instructs people well in peace, and by the time he is done, Nemo has killed just as surely as if his aims had been bad.

The sea closes over both men.

But Ahab dead is doomed just as he was doomed alive.

While hope lives on after Nemo when, through either remorse or inadvertency, he puts his ship down into the maelstrom. We are unsure of his death.

On the last page of his book, Verne offers us this thought:

If [the *Nautilus* has survived] and if Captain Nemo still inhabits the ocean—the country of his adoption—

then may the hatred be appeased in his savage heart! May the contemplation of so many wonders extinguish in him the spirit of revenge! May the judge disappear and the scientist continue his peaceful exploration of the seas! However strange his destiny may be, it is also sublime!

And in that sublimity lies hope for Nemo and his American nephews, the boys who have grown to manhood and machinery since.

For Ahab the hope would be meaningless. If by some miracle Melville's madman should open his cold eyes at the sea bottom, the contemplation of Verne's rainbow wonders would but drive him deeper into his own abyss. Melville's maelstrom, sucking down through the gorge of Ahab's soul, could swallow Verne's toy *Nautilus* whole.

But swallow it it never will.

For what we have examined here are two ways of looking at the world. Ages alternate with doses of despair and tonics of survival. Some ages balance between. We are given choices. Some ages do not choose and thus lose ground in the great vote taking of time and the deliverance of power either into or out of their hands.

One hundred years ago, this yea-sayer and this naysayer, literarily anyway, offered us the choice of the nodded or the shaken head. Separated by thousands of sea miles, yet cheek by jowl, these authors represented two halves of the newly emergent American attitude toward the world and debated whether to live under nature's thunderbolts and rainstorms; accept, tolerate, as all had done before.

One decided to give God as good as He got and stormed heaven as if it were hell.

The other favored pacing God, running at His elbow,

recharging man's batteries, using His juice, so as to later circumvent Him with newer, brighter machineries of sacrilege. These devices saved men's lives when God said die, they reared sick men tall whilst God said fall down dead, lie cold.

And now that we are well into this age of electronics and have begun to worry about how to let some new kind of God concept back in through even so much as a side door, we shall witness the pendulum swing, quite often, between Ahab and Nemo. On successive days we may feel tempted to either utter destruction or utter mechanical creativity or combinations and variations on both.

If I assay right, we in America are just emerging from a period inclining toward the Melvillean. We are tempted to hurl our sick heart into God's face.

But I think instead we should listen to the good and reassuring beat of the circuiting mechanical pump in our hospitals, where man's salt blood bypasses his failing heart to be aerated and returned to his waiting and hopeful body. The medical machines of our time, throbbing, would have seemed music to Verne. They calm the ravening intellect that would run too fast to change the world, perhaps by disaster.

The world *will* change, at any rate, through outright fury, neglect, or through the mild but dedicated blasphemy of such as Nemo.

Ahab might explode a hydrogen bomb to shake the foundations of God.

But in the fright-flash of illumination, at some distance, we would see Nemo reperusing notes made in mathematical symbols to use such energy to send men to the stars rather than scatter them in green milk glass and radioactive chaff along the shore.

These, then, are the captains of our American soul. We

could choose between them, if we wished, as tomorrow's light comes in the window.

Decide that God has joined the universe with warped and spokeless wheels, and so take Melville and invite the abyss.

Decide that *man's* architecture is in sore need of retrials and testings, and so put in with Mr. Verne.

The latter might be our greatest temptation, for we have always resembled Nemo rather more than Ahab.

We have always been the American Boy Mechanic, his cellar full of homemade helicopters, his attic chocked with canvas batwings, an unfinished rowboat in the basement, a bicycle-built-for-two-hovercraft in the yard.

America was ingenuity. It still is and could be. Spit, string, and tinfoil once our girded armor and the grand dream our goal, we have too often now folded our money into our pockets and strolled off while doom bided its time and wetted its whistle around the corner.

So, surprisingly enough, the book you hold in your hands is more than timely, as are all of Verne's books. Remarkable not so much for what he predicted—and he predicted much, gave bones to boys on which to skin their dreams—but because of its attitude, American in the best sense, that we can somehow make do somewhere, anywhere, if we collect our spit, save our string, and ball our tinfoil.

Melville wrote to Hawthorne of *Moby Dick*, "I have written an evil book."

Similarly, seen from other days and ways, Verne might have written some literary friend that yesterday's evil can be hammered into today's good, yesterday's provocation to morality can be rechanneled toward survival in tomorrow.

The logic that informs Ahab's madness destroys him.

The logic that informs Nemo can well build us homes on far

planets circling more safely placed suns. Like Nemo, we may well find we need not destroy the horrific whale of reality; we may lurk inside it with machineries, plotting our destinies and going our terror-fraught ways toward an hour when we can lie under those stranger suns and bask easy and breathe light and know peace.

We will probably not choose between these writers but carry both with us into the future. We will have need of one to question blind matter and the other to cross-examine blind man. Thus fused, we shall face the future with fortitude and stamina.

But before we move up in seas of space, the time is now to move sidewise and along and down through seas of water. Here, then, is Verne's *20,000 Leagues Under the Sea*, his "American" book, his book "moderne," his particular sublime and mad captain, and his strange metal fish.

Portholes tight! Periscope down!

Prepare to submerge.

THAT FUTURE WITH A FUNNY NAME (1995)

How do you spell the future to make sure it happens in the right way?

How do you stop 1984 from ever arriving?

How do you freeze Big Brother in his tracks?

It has always seemed to me that while the politicians are hoisting themselves up in their hot-air balloons with no ballast, going nowhere, you run along ahead of them and . . .

Invent the future, build it while no one is looking. Dream the cliché-impossible-dream that everyone doubts and no one believes in until they wind up next door to or surrounded by it and, too late, they're in love.

Go ahead and smile, laugh quietly even, as I change the name, date and place of Orwell's 1984 with:

Wimberly, Allison, Tong & Goo.

No, I'm not writing and sending this from Hyperbole, Kansas.

I have seen the future, and it is more than a promised land, and we don't have to march there; it is near at hand, its roots are in Southern California, and its gardens are across the world.

I expect at this point you will heave a great sigh of gloom and doom, slam this book shut, and hurl it across the room. But wait. How did I come to this uncomfortable position, this glorious view of tomorrow morning?

Prepare yourself for coincidence.

I did some minor consulting work on the Orbitron ride at

Euro Disney outside Paris, a few years ago. Attending the opening-day ceremonies, in the late afternoon I went up to the second floor of the Disneyland Hotel to sit with a cold beer and a fine view of the new park, musing on its many qualities.

Halfway through my drink, a stranger walked up with his wife and asked permission to sit at my table. I agreed, amiably, and we chatted for a few minutes about the park, the happy celebration, and tonight's fireworks. I looked around at the hotel and praised it, saying it was very fine.

"But," I added, "I know a hotel finer than this. The greatest, to me anyway, hotel in the world, and I've lived in dozens of them!"

"What hotel is that?" said the stranger.

"The Grand Floridian, at Disney World, Florida," I said, working up steam. "Everything about it invites. The shape, the size, the colors, the restaurants. And the main lobby, which rises at least six floors above the conversational area below and gives kids notions about running up there to circle 'round and think about spitting down at their parents below. What a place! The Grand Floridian. Go there!"

"I've been," said the stranger. "That's mine."

"Yours?"

"Ours, I should say. Our architectural firm in Newport, California."

"My God!" I cried. "And here I've been shooting off my mouth . . . !"

"It's all right," said Gerald Allison, reaching out to shake my hand, laughing. "Don't stop."

I haven't. I'm still saying the same, only more so. Since then I've stayed again at the Grand Floridian and see no reason to change. I'd still like to run up to the sixth floor to sail paper planes or spit. I always leave there a foot shorter and ten times louder than when I came through the door.

Needless to say, Gerry Allison and I started the swiftest friendship in history that afternoon. And I haven't changed my mind about him or his cohorts since. Little did I know that when I shook his hand, I was shaking the hand of a kid who once dreamed of clearing the jungle to fast-find a lost city. This was my blood brother, raised late nights on awful radio shows and reading *Tarzan and the City of Gold* with a flashlight, totally forbidden, under the covers halfway toward morn.

So what you have here are not, as they claim, postcards of the future. They are good promises that can and will be kept.

Wimberly, Allison, Tong & Goo, like Gaul, exists in four parts, but the four parts make a whole that can lick the bejesus out of a small part of the future.

Can Gerry and his pals solve and improve everything? No way. But they can nibble and nick and munch around the edges of time and, bit by bit, change cities that have fallen to skeleton and skin, and make viral implants in dead tissue to watch long-dormant towns revitalize themselves, said viruses giving life rather than taking it.

Politics seem to have no cure for our empty boulevards and parks, but corporate cash and architectural imagination can guarantee at least safe walking and living places. Schweitzer once said, Do something good, someone may imitate it. Allison and Associates can, then, set examples, near cities if not in them, to be seen and imitated.

While a good part of Africa self-destroys, Wimberly, Allison, Tong & Goo discovers a civilization that never was and promise a future not over the rainbow but underfoot. I would go there, to their bee-loud glades.

Big Brother will never be dead.

But they're giving him a rough time.

HYSTERIA, GODDESS OF FLIGHT, OR ON TAKEOFF, DO *NOT* RUN UP AND DOWN THE AISLES SCREAMING (1993)

Everyone knows, of course, that I do not fly, have never flown, and have no immediate plans for such madness.

That is my myth.

But at last the truth must come out.

After sixty-two years, my romantic, if cowardly, image must be shattered.

I have been flying secretly, and not so secretly, for one hundred and twenty months.

Before that, Stan Freberg planned to star me in an advertisement, stepping into a jet. I was fooled into doing so by the fact that the airline had pasted a gigantic papier-mâché painting of a locomotive over the jet's body while the pilot, in a train engineer's cap, waved a lantern out the window, causing me to think I was boarding the Superchief.

None of that, now.

On October 17, 1982, propelled by three double martinis, I took off ahead of my jet, bound for L.A.

But that's the *end* of my story.

What came first? How did I unknot my viscera and, egged on by some loony minor god of high winds and low morale, let myself be carried, writhing, onto a cross-country flight?

It all began with my traveling by train, my usual tourist's mode or venue (to use the latest "in" word). I arrived to lecture in New Orleans, prepared to head south to Orlando the next day for the grand opening of Epcot at Disney World. I had been a creative writer and consultant on its main Gulliver-size Spaceship Earth. I was to join dozens of cocreators for a three-day multimillion-dollar send-off.

On arriving in New Orleans, what did I find? That Amtrak, in an act of brilliant ineptitude, had canceled all future train travel from Chicago to New Orleans to Orlando. The most-traveled, most-populated train system in the U.S.A. was shot dead in its tracks. In order to visit mid-Florida, I would have to entrain for Washington, D.C., and triangulate back to Miami. "Washington, D.C.!" I cried. "Do you mean to say I have to go where I don't want to go in order to ricochet back south!?"

I ordered a limousine and an old colored chauffeur. He wasn't black, no, no. He was colored and old, somewhere in his seventies, and moved and talked like the old semidark retainers in childhood films.

We set out for Orlando and never arrived. Along the way God whispered, "Fly, dummy!" A few moments later, we blew a tire in the middle of the freeway.

Well, now. When was the last time you changed an automobile tire?

When was the last time, for that matter, that you changed the tire on an elephantine limousine?

When was the last time you changed an elephantine limousine tire in the middle of a freeway with cars shrieking by at sixty or seventy miles per hour?

When was the last time you got the spare tire out of the limousine trunk only to find that there was only an hour's worth of tread on same?

And, finally, when was the last time you went searching to buy a spare tire for that great big limousine in and around and through Tallahassee?

Right. You got the picture.

It took about three hours of touching in and out of gas and tire stations, treating our spare tread gingerly, before we found a shop that took one look at the Martian visitor and his retainer and overcharged us for the last elephantine tire within reach. And all the while, God, leaning over my left shoulder, kept muttering, "Fly, dummy!"

With the new tire in place and no spare in the trunk, since we had bought the last similar tire in a hundred miles, we headed south again.

The dear Lord kept reasonably silent until around four in the afternoon, when he repeated his celestial advice and—

The limousine engine rolled over stone cold and played dead elephant.

No kicking, no reasoning, no oiling, no gassing, no cursing could cause the prone or perhaps even supine beast to rouse. We glided by happenstance into the courtyard of a not-very-festive-looking Holiday Inn, where the limo stuttered the last lines of Caesar dying and assumed rigor mortis. I had to restrain my retainer from putting a bullet behind the engine block.

"It is the final night of the World Series," I reasoned. "Let us rent a cheap room with two six-packs of expensive beer and drink toasts to a complete loss of memory."

I retired to do just that and watched the Series with much dubiety until the third Coors, which made the Series look ten times better than it was. Who was playing that night? Silly. Did I sleep well, even though I heard my chauffeur rampaging in, under, and on top of the funereal creature? You betcha.

The next morning my chauffeur reported that he was threatening the limo with the junkyard but so far had had no response. There was no use my hanging around for a prognosis.

Why didn't I call a local taxicab and buy four hundred dollars' worth of travel to Orlando?

Checking my wallet, I heard our dear Lord repeating his litany about skies, wings, travel, and time.

The local taxi—there was only one in the nameless town nearby—arrived driven by the town sheriff, a near relative of the law in *Smokey and the Bandit*.

Well, sir, I got the complete tour, on all sides in every community, proclaimed by the sheriff as we dusted the miles, of which ditch held the town drunks, where the ladies or women or girls of ill-after-midnight repute might be unearthed, and how many unlucky ones had been bruised or dashed to a finality on this particular stretch of highway. By the time we reached Orlando, I had the whole history of northern Florida in one ear, winding its way with a thick southern accent out the other. I said not a word, seeing as how it was my true encounter with a chicken-fried keeper of the law. He chanted facts as easily as a pachinko game spills its miniballs. I enjoyed being out in his rain.

I hated saying good-bye to the sheriff, but there was important business. Listening to my Maker yet one more time, I flung myself into the arms of the Disney people and cried, "Feed me three double martinis, buy me a ticket, and fly me home in a jet!"

There you have it. The moment you have been waiting for. The collapse of my morale. The ruination of my myth: a lifetime of catching trolleys, buses, and trains. As I babbled my desire to the Disney folks, I stared at the sky and wondered:

Will I ever travel at twice the speed of sound?

A frisson of premonition chilled my shoulder blades where tiny ice crystals budded and burst forth in wings.

I had three long and most joyful days to brood over Kitty

Hawk, bastard son of the Wright Brothers' decision. Three days in which the gates of Epcot were flung open and thousands of special invitees from all over the world rode with me back through time and up into the future in Spaceship Earth, whose interior architecture I had prefigured with words, consulting with Disney, three years before. Three days of Harry James, Lionel Hampton and his vibes, youth bands, late-night Larry King talk shows, and a million bucks' worth of fireworks delivered me at last to Day of the Birdman.

Yes, yes, you mutter, but when was it you stopped being afraid?

Not that day.

The Disney people had warned the Orlando airport folks that they were toting me into Guillotine Seven, removing my shoes to lessen the drag.

Shocked at the incredible news, more than one airline official was there to help me off the tumbrel. I *think* it was more than one official. After the first martini, they moved around a lot. I must add, I really don't *like* martinis. But the immense jar they provided was called a Quick Fix, so I relented. It was then that the extra officials appeared out of nowhere, joking about my fear of crashing. They did *not* say crash-*landing*, you may notice. They gave me jovial punches in the arm to welcome me to my new age of heaven-inspired freedom. They noted but did not comment on the fresh chalk-white pallor of my usually pumpkin-colored cheeks. The jokes continued, the martinis de-iced my hidden wings, and once I was in a fluid state, not unlike mercury skimming the surface of a cold plate, they siphoned me in the general direction of the jet. As I lurched into my seat, they offered me a belt. No thanks, I said, I've already had six! No, no, they said, around your middle, and tightened me in. Someone was whispering prayers to a passenger, unlisted, named Mary. That's all right, I thought, go right ahead, even though I'm a Baptist!

The airline officials put a Boy Scout knot in my belt, bussed me on both cheeks, and bade me what sounded like a truly final farewell.

A radio voice advised that I must keep my seat belt on during the *entire* voyage.

"Don't worry!" I said.

Some stranger came by and asked if I wanted to sit by the window.

"Not necessarily," I said.

"I'll tell you when we fly over the Mississippi," someone else said.

"I'd rather not know," I said.

The flight attendant asked, "What would you like to drink after takeoff?"

"What've you *got*?" I said. Then, "Anything," I added, like a good sport.

"There are small paper bags, right there," said a nurse—I think that's what they called her—standing over me.

"I'll take three," I said.

"It's all in your mind," the amiable lady said.

"Yes, but it wants *out*," I said.

"Sit back and relax," she said.

I tightened myself into a ball, and we took off.

No, wait. First there were three hours of warming the engines. *Then* the takeoff.

"The most dangerous time," someone behind me said, "is taking off and landing."

I wish we could do both and get it over with, I thought.

But, for the time being, we went in one direction: up!

We were airborne!

And suddenly the aisles were full of people. Not running up and down and screaming, no, but laughing quietly and patting my head or giving me hugs. I had been so busy with my private panics that I hadn't noticed I was surrounded by Disney people returning to California after the Big Celebratory Bang. Animators, architectural consultants, storyboard specialists, musicians, composers, conductors, watercolorists, vice presidents—they all came by to say, "There, there, Ray, it's okay. We're in charge. We'll keep the plane up."

Did I stare down at the Rocky Mountains as we flew over? Nope.

Did I witness the Grand Canyon from forty thousand feet? Not really.

Did I look out at the five-hundred-square-mile spread of Los Angeles by night and all those millions of lights?

The lady next to me described it.

"I would rather not hear," I finally said.

Did I run to the bathroom just once during the entire five-hour trip?

You've got to be kidding!

In any event, I and my mob of mobile Disney psychologists made it across the perfectly friendly skies of someone else's airline for a blind landing at LAX. Blind meaning me, of course, with my eyes shut, praying that the pilots had theirs open.

Another airline official was there to greet me. He held a bottle of Mumm's in his hands. I feared he might crack it across my prow and christen me Child of Lucky Lindy out of Earhart. Before I could move, I seized the champagne while the *Time* magazine photographers' cameras flashed at me in my seat, white-knuckled the armrests, and kept muttering, "Is it back, is it back?"

"Is what back?" the *Time* people said.

"The earth," I said, eyes shut.

They must've looked out the window. "Yup," they said. "There it is."

"Take me out there where I can feel it," I said.

I did not kiss the tarmac. Knowing that the pope would want to do that in later years, I refrained.

So far, so good. My conversion to the sky did not start on that day, but it grew over a period of months and years. I did not fly again for a year, and then gradually I took jets at three-month and then two-month and then one-month intervals.

And one morning about two years ago, it finally happened. I took off as a nonbeliever and landed sober.

That was the giveaway. I looked down at my empty hand and nonexistent glass.

Holy moly! I thought. I've stopped drinking!

A small lightbulb did not switch on in my brain. To put it mildly, a Bible-size Revelation crash-landed between my ears and skidded to a halt in a surf of fire-repellent foam.

I was not afraid of *flying*!

No, not at all.

All those years I'd been fearful of, frightened of, terrified by . . . *me*.

Playing Medusa to myself, every time I envisioned me flying, I froze myself in place.

It was *me* all the time!

Not the jet, the sky, the flight, the takeoff, or the landing.

But that shortly after takeoff, I might bound up with a yell and go screaming down the aisles, out of control.

That I would babble, "Stop everything, hold 'er, Newt, this milquetoast wants out!"

Commensurate with ordering a rowboat and waving bye to the *Queen Elizabeth II* in mid-Atlantic.

In my dreams I had seen myself leaping over legs, spilling drinks, and shrieking, "Whose idea *was* this?!"

And someone tying a wet sheet over me.

I gazed at that image of myself for a long time and then murmured, "I'll be damned. So *that's* it?"

And after a while, *not* ordering any martinis for the flight, I began to laugh.

There you have it at last. Not much of a story perhaps, but my own.

That first flight was in October 1982. Since then I have made thirty flights across country and fifteen flights on the Concorde to Paris. If I drink at all, it is some of those fine French or equally fine California wines.

So?

So look in the mirror. Maybe your fear was once mine. Maybe you're playing Medusa to yourself and are frozen in place with a shriek locked under your tongue and no deicer.

Maybe.

Meanwhile, I wish someone would buy me a license. And teach me to drive.

TIME TO EXPLORE AGAIN: WHERE IS THE MADMAN WHO'LL TAKE US TO MARS? (2004)

In this time when our freeways are frozen in place, space travel suffers the same terrible winter. Years have passed since *Apollo 11*, with only faint cries for a lunar rediscovery, then Mars and beyond.

How can we thaw this deep freeze to unlock our vision so that we see the stars once more with the same fever that we knew that fabulous night we took the first Giant Step?

Let's look at the situation five hundred years ago.

Columbus, financed by Spain's royalty, sailed for India. King Henry VIII, jealous, paid Giovanni Caboto (John Cabot) to track Columbus. Francis I of France, thus provoked, hired Verrazano to do the same. Of the three, only Verrazano made landfall at what became Kitty Hawk. Incredible! Verrazano sailed west, and five centuries on, the Wright Brothers soared east to explore space and time.

There was, then, a confluence of kings who sent their ships to spice and gold. Today there is no such desire in our Congress or our president for similar goals.

What must happen next?

Can Science Fiction writers, inspirers of futures, cause a seed change in the American imagination so that, in turn, our leaders can be influenced? For remember when Admiral Byrd touched the North Pole, he cried, "Jules Verne leads me!" Where are the Jules Vernes, alive today to change our ways?

Let me make a list of some possible alternatives. Why not encourage our original competitor, Russia, to get back in the chase?

Signs indicate that there's a slow return to Communist authority, which might well mean not only authoritarian politics that kept millions in bondage, but also the arrogance which caused them to circumnavigate space with Gagarin. Properly provoked and still aggravated at our "Tear down the wall," might they not desire to beat us to Mars?

Or consider our two great enemies/friends. Germany, after all, lost two wars at our hands. France was saved from those two wars by our help. There's every reason for those two nations to hate us.

Why not irritate some new Wernher von Braun in Berlin to invent a Mars rocket and beat us to a landing? And the French, stung by their defeats and the salvation we offered, mightn't they want to send a foreign legion to the deserts of Mars?

And yet again Japan, an American-conquered nation, remembering the intrusion of Admiral Perry in Tokyo Harbor. And from the ruins of Hiroshima, might they not send a rocket to touch Phobos and Deimos and move beyond Mars to Centauri?

Or perhaps Canada, that invisible nation, ignored for centuries. Might they, in a macho gesture, fling themselves into space?

Or, most incredible of all, imagine that the Vatican decided that Pope John III wished to build a spacecraft titled the *Holy Ghost* in order to fly across the universe in search of the beginnings of Creation. With the Moon as base and Mars as second manger, that pope might move on to study the wellsprings of the cosmos.

What, then, would be the effect on our prejudiced secular America? Would we not build a bigger, better, and almost more holy rocket to follow the ecclesiastical dusts?

Or what if the Muslims . . . ?

But no, perish the thought.

Put all these together, shove them in tomorrow's slot machine, and pull the handle. If the totals come up with three swastikas, three hammer and sickles, or three papal crowns with honeybee insignia, the results may well be the same.

What we need now is a competition of hatreds and loves. The final reward on Mars might well be not spices or gold, but the squashing of egos and a promise of immortality.

In any event, time is running out. Congress, as usual, is imitating Sleeping Beauty. It is time to waken from the slumber.

That footprint on the Moon is being filled with eternal dust and Mars still waits to have its canals filled with our dreams. Where, oh where, is the technological madman to wake us from our slumbers and provide us with the proper destiny?

Tomorrow morning, may that madman be born.

ABOUT PARIS

PARIS: ALWAYS DESTROYED, ALWAYS TRIUMPHANT (1986)

Let me tell you a somewhat lengthy story.

Recently my wife and I traveled to Paris again, where friends asked us what we were doing there. We replied, "We have come to celebrate your failed revolution."

At which point there was a terrible silence among our Parisian friends. Before they could haul off and hit me, I proceeded to explain.

"Well, didn't your revolution fail? You wound up two hundred years ago with the Terror, you inherited Napoleon, Lafayette was imprisoned in Holland and had to be released through a letter from George Washington. You then moved on into the nineteenth century with a series of new, smaller, failed revolutions, the reestablishment of the king and the failure of the king, the Commune in Paris in 1870 when you fought the Germans outside the city and yourselves inside the city, and all was a failure. Then in 1914 you lost that war, and we had to come rescue you. In 1940 you lost a war again, and we had to come over with Patton and Montgomery and de Gaulle to save your face. Isn't it wonderful that in the face of all this despair, all this failure, you seized forth the most beautiful country in the world and the most beautiful city, Paris?"

At which point my French friends lunged forward, grasped me in a rib-cracking hug, and gave me multitudinous kisses. All was well.

And indeed it is strange that out of such a terrible history, this magnificent country and this incredible city were born.

I return to Paris each year, if possible on Bastille Day, so I can go up on the Eiffel Tower and watch the city explode with fireworks.

If I were to advise you as a tourist on what to do the first day or the first week in the city, it would be to stroll alone, with no others, across Paris, stopping every half hour at an outdoor café to have a coffee or a beer or an aperitif, and carry under your arm a copy of F. Scott Fitzgerald's *Tender Is the Night*. Every year when I go back, I do not take a copy of Fitzgerald's book— I always buy a new one and write in it: *"Paris, 1998," "1999,"* or *"2000."* I have a number of copies of *Tender Is the Night* on my shelf at home to remind me of my excursions in the great city. It strikes me as the perfect novel to read in the ambience of that great environment.

If you stand in front of Notre-Dame and look to your left, you will see a street that's no more than an alley that extends for the good part of a mile. If you enter this alley and walk from one end to the other, you will encounter at least six hundred restaurants. On each block there are thirty restaurants on one side and thirty on the other. And so it goes, all the way down to the boulevard Saint-Michel and beyond.

The business of Paris is eating, as it should be for every city of the world that counts as a city. Paris has twenty thousand restaurants, and so in any direction that you move, you are surrounded by millions of people outdoors, eating, in even the middle of winter.

My wife and I were in Paris at the time of the great soccer matches with international teams. On the Thursday before we were to leave, France was victorious over Croatia. From our hotel window, we saw the beginning of madness. The city was stirring alive in mobs to celebrate this wonderful victory. We had to leave the next day, Saturday, to return by Concorde to the United States. I arrived back in L.A. late Saturday night, and the next day was to be the final between France and Brazil. I had to go to the desert and have never learned to drive, so when I went out of L.A. I hired a limousine, in the back of which was a television set. I never use such devices when I travel—I always find the scenery of greater interest—but on this particular day in the afternoon, Paris, across the world, was combating Brazil. I suddenly remembered the words I had spoken to my dear friends in France: "From the history of failure, you have snatched success." And so as I watched France with its long history of lost wars, I could not help but speak over and over again, "Oh, please, God, let them win. They haven't won a war in two hundred years. Let them battle well, and let there be a great triumph this day that will make the entire country go mad, at last, with the knowledge that they have accomplished something with such a terrible history behind them." The encounter went on, and I became more nervous and began to shout in my mind, and finally, at the end of the game, France won. On TV I witnessed a country gone terribly wild with joy, because at long last, at the end of too many years, a war had been won and France could arise from the ashes in triumph. So much for France, so much for Paris. Bastille night all over again, but an even better Bastille.

THE SIXTY-MINUTE LOUVRE: PARIS BY STOPWATCH (1993)

If you had no other choice, would you tour the Louvre in sixty minutes, no more, no less?

Perhaps a dumb question, but in life we are often forced to do things that, on normal days, we would refuse.

Another question: What if you were a traveler from a far place and someone offered you one single chance to see Paris, but only for ninety minutes?

What if you knew you might never return again, so you had best take the opportunity, risk the chance, and see the fabulous French city in just five thousand four hundred seconds?

Or imagine that you have been dead for a few hundred years and God comes to you in your long sleep and says, I will gift you with the most incredible place of places, but only for one hour and a half. Called back to life, to Paris, would you refuse?

I would not. I could not. I did not.

Years ago, I had to make the swift decision. Traveling from Calais to Paris to Rome by train, I arrived at dusk one April evening in a sleeping car with a private room. On board the train with me were my friend Lord Kilbracken and his girlfriend. When they learned there was to be a ninety-minute stopover for me in Paris before I trained on to Italy, they begged me to leave my luggage on board and come with them for a quick dinner before racing across Paris to catch my train. Fearful, I refused. They argued and won! With great doubt I abandoned my train at six o'clock that night, and we took a taxicab across Paris to Les Deux Magots.

Paris and the twilight seized and held me immediately. It was the blue hour, the hour of enchantment. As we motored past the Louvre, it was painted ancient gold by the sun. Every leaf on every bush or every tree was bronzed with twilight illumination. As we rounded the Place de la Concorde, to our right the Church of the Madeleine was a fiery temple, and yet farther on as we rushed, the Arc de Triomphe burned with fading light and the Eiffel Tower was a great pure torch that showed our way to where we vanished along the way to sitting out in the cool dusk drinking aperitifs at Les Deux Magots.

By that time I was exhilarated and in tears: I had died and been delivered to a place of golden coins that minted themselves by the tens of thousands from gods' mouths in fountains. All of the talk I heard, though I understood none of it, was wise and mythical and rare. All of the people walked or sat with faces bright and colored into masks by the last of the sun. The drink in my hand was a vintage two thousand years old. Among legions of young men, I thought I saw Caesar stride by in his pride! My friends, seated with me, were dipped in gilt and capable of living forever.

But time was passing.

Already it was six-thirty. We had but an hour to find a small bistro and devour a meal. Just down the street and in a small alley, we found the amazing chicken and a wine from the tomb of a king somehow preserved to give wits to our tongues. We could not help but to speak now Camus, now Molière, now Voltaire-Berlitz!

But suddenly the golden light was gone, the chicken devoured, the bottle empty. Our time was up! It was seven o'clock!

Only thirty minutes in which to find a cab and catch my precious train!

With sudden panic we paid the bill and rushed along the streets shouting, waving. No taxis anywhere! Or if there were, they were full, while still others, empty, refused to stop!

Five minutes, ten minutes, fifteen minutes passed in madness as the three of us waved, shouted, despaired. I imagined my luggage leaving without me as the train roared off.

But, at last, a taxicab. We leaped in with great shouts of relief and sped through a Paris still faintly radiant with torches long ago carried up from Rome.

At the railroad station, my train was slowly beginning to move! I yelled, fled from my friends and leaped aboard only in time. Eyes brimming with relief and joy I shall recall forever, I waved to my friends, who diminished away in the twilight and Paris into a special past.

I stood in the window for a long while, savoring the wine and the silhouettes of Paris sinking into a river of night. I knew that I had been privileged by accident or by my friends' design to enjoy a most particular, if peculiar, Paris by stopwatch. I would come back in later years again and again, but it would never be a similar special adventure as impromptu, as silly, as lovely as this had been.

I had been challenged to a race, or I had fallen victim to a folly, or God had wakened me from a long morbidity of sleep and handed me those ninety minutes to do with as I wished. I had answered the call, run the folly, drunk the wine, and now? I was immensely happy.

I do not recommend my journey to everyone. But sometimes, late at night, I am on that train again and I arrive and Paris is waiting in an amazing light like dawn, and I cry out in my sleep, glad for those five thousand four hundred seconds of special time, and then I wake up, happy to remember. What if I had never come back to Paris? Would the ninety-minute memory serve for the rest of my life to enhance my dreams? It would have to, yes?

Let us imagine, then, that God and a sour travel guide fire off a gun to propel us in and out of the Louvre at full jog, remembering that Bernard Berenson, the great Italian Renaissance historian, warned his friends, year on year, to spend no more than an hour in any museum. Not even ninety minutes, mind you! Sixty! Beyond that, he warned, the eyes gum, the limbs collapse, the mind sleeps. Get out! he said.

With Berenson in full trot to arrive promptly and leave early, what confronts us at the Louvre?

Two roadblocks. The outer pyramid, the inner smile.

Unlike some Parisians who hated Pei's crystal architecture sight unseen, I welcomed it. For it is the bright headstone on those best-of-all-possible-world treasures buried here: memories of obelisks, one seen on the way across the Place de la Concorde, plus the ghosts of Napoleon, Champollion, Denon, and three thousand Egyptian years. So Pei's pyramid is a great lantern over a sandstorm Nile River past.

I descend to find . . .

The second roadblock, the smile that haunts until, with a sigh, you go to kowtow to *The Mona Lisa*, pretend adoration, and leave. Yes, yes. I know! Da Vinci lugged her on horseback to meet, create, and die with Francis I. But the phantasmal face of Leonardo's Virgin of the Rocks erases the smile.

Standing before her, I recall a story I wrote forty years ago in which future anarchists defile Da Vinci's portrait, rip it apart. One piece is saved by a ten-year-old boy, who sneaks home at midnight. As the moon rises, he opens his clenched fist to find, safely buried there: the smile.

All that being true, I do not prolong my visit with Mona Lisa. Blasphemous, yes, but off I go.

Swiftly I pass Monet, Manet, Hals, Boucher, Seurat, even Fra Angelico. For I must rush to meet my true lifetime love!

Why this headlong flight from yesteryear's painters and paintings?

Champollion and Denon call. I run, with children in my wake.

Why ignore the Louvre in its immensity to stare at Karnak, weep at Thebes?

Those very children, of course. Isn't the problem of enticing the young getting them to even enter a gallery door? Guided, do they not sleepwalk and cry, "Are we *there* yet?"

If their destination is the mummies that we all love, grinning beneath their linen sheaths, yes.

For consider, most of us entering any museum, anywhere, enter to move in ignorance. We know not the pictures nor the names. But children?! Which means all of us. From early on we are immersed in Nile waters. When we see Tut photographed, we wave! We stuff ourselves with pyramid funerals, Sphinx profiles, pictographed sarcophagi—all that *good* stuff. By osmosis we grow into our tenth year ready for the Louvre catacombs where Thutmose and Nefertiti stay. Time later to rise from that dust-that-is-spice to half wake with Boucher and David. Now with the wisdom of children whose nightly dreams are cat and jackal gods, we obey the primal urge to lose ourselves in antiquities.

But first—dim the lights.

I have always fancied a museum lurked in after midnight. To stand in darkness, to pick out spectral shapes by candle or flash . . . ah, that's the best! No stranger's elbow stabbing your ribs, no docent mobs when you want to stray, wander, touch or even whisper to Ramses' or Cleopatra's friends. No civilization in all history could appreciate my midnight séances more than the Egyptians.

So as the museum night-lights extinguish, follow my tour of four thousand years and forty thousand dynastic artifacts. None brought here by Napoleon—his were long since seized for transport to British museums. Including the fabulously evocative Sèvres Egyptian dinner service that Napoleon presented to Josephine and which bored her, mysteriously. I have future plans to snatch it from London's Apsley House to table it here as service for the waiting pharaohs in the hungry tombs.

If Napoleon, then, and his dinnerware are not here, very little abides of Denon, who accompanied Bonaparte. Champollion, who came later, accomplished more.

What *is* here would cargo a thousand Nile skiffs:

The bronze statue of Karomama, brought back from Egypt by Champollion, who then purchased the statue of Ramses II plus a hundred sarcophagi, two hundred sculptures in marble, and two thousand sculptures in bronze, the largest collection that exists outside of Egypt. Plus the crypt of Osiris with animal mummies and sarcophagi and the crypt of the Sphinx, containing a colossal Sphinx and two statues in relief representing King Ramses II adoring the god Horus, plus the meals and menus for pharaohs on their death-boat journeys.

Sixty minutes isn't half enough for this Egyptian eternity.

Having swum the Nile past to arrive in the postimpressionist present, your children along with myself are perhaps now open to meeting Toulouse-Lautrec, Gauguin, and Cézanne.

Time now to scout out the occasional Daumier, the almost forgotten Doré, and the not-often-enough-mentioned

Grandville, if such can be searched for and found here in the endless caches and bins. Time now to refeather the wings of the Victory and fit imaginary arms to the Milo Venus. And then, why not? Go back to confront Mona Lisa to see if our sojourn with mummified cats and canopic jars stuffed with royal tripes has improved her disposition. Because of our trafficking with tombs, has her mouth shaped to a warmer smile? Perhaps.

I end my lightning tour as I began thirty-nine years ago when I circuited Paris to pause for a moment before this museum.

Today the view is the same but with the addition of the crystal pyramid behind me as celebratory cap to the buried wonders.

Three years ago at twilight, I stood gazing along the Tuileries, the Place de la Concorde, and on up to the Arc. With my camera I snapped three dozen photos in what I often describe as the David Lean hour, that golden time before night when that film director, waiting for inspired illumination, caught his subjects painted with illusory gold. For this view of Paris, I thank the raw fact that the outer galleries of the Louvre were left unfinished, leaving the panorama all the way to the Tour Eiffel to stun visitors like myself who arrive for ninety minutes but stay a lifetime.

So we have ascended out of Paris into Paris, out of France into France, out of the weather of old time into a weather of the always incredible present, having been rained on by history.

ABOUT LOS ANGELES

QUEEN OF ANGELS, NOT QUITE READY FOR HER CLOSE-UP (UNDATED)

Last night I saw upon the stair
An Angel Queen that wasn't there.
She wasn't there again today.
My God, I wish she'd go away.

In other words: L.A., now you see her, now you don't.

The Queen of Angels is three separate cities, none of which is L.A., but all share the territory.

Listen up.

I love to breakfast in oceanside Malibu, head in to a snow-mountain lunch at Lake Arrowhead, careen down for a Palm Springs desert dinner, then double back to Los Angeles for a midnight snack.

Thus ignoring L.A. itself, for in between these three civilizations there is a desolation.

Hollywood Boulevard for mindless years has had no Hollywood and Vine.

World visitors hoping to glimpse Tinseltown's navel find only Gertrude Stein's: "There's no *there* there."

When a New York photography team flew in years ago to film the famed intersection they panicked, finding nothing.

"Go find it at Disney World!" I said. "Walt's elves snatched Hollywood and Vine one night and flew it to Florida, along with every rare Hollywood Boulevard building I roller-skated past as a kid."

Now at the west end of Hollywood, they are erecting a giant fortress/cathedral/cinema near Grauman's Chinese for next year's Oscars. From this grand embankment, film moguls can ignore the homeless peasants on desolate Hollywood Boulevard waiting for Quasimodo's downpour of bricks and hot lead.

The rest of Hollywood, from twenty years of neglect, will be a graveyard rarely visited after sundown. The entire street needs resurrection, but the humungous cathedral opens next spring.

Similarly on downtown Los Angeles's Broadway at sunset, all pedestrians have fled. Chinatown is abandoned, gangs roam free, so the best cafés have turned off their ovens.

The old billboards of Columbia and RKO Studios on Gower Street stand empty. Nothing has been done to revitalize these landmarks to give tourist buses a passing sense of history.

The saddest night in recent history was New Year's Eve 2000, when TV cameras exploded with mobs and fireworks in wild Paris, New York, and Rome, only to fizzle in L.A. when a sparse assembly of Angelenos huddled under the huge HOLLY-WOOD sign with their beanbags and kazoos. The worldwide cameras turned off in disbelief.

There is hope in the arrival of new mayor Hahn, who has a greater sympathy for what cities are.

Meanwhile, to enjoy Los Angeles you must prowl those malls that duplicate the old dreams of what L.A. once was.

Beyond that, you must sift the rich sands of Malibu, ski Lake Arrowhead snows, and broil in the Palm Springs sun. In between, the old Queen of Angels is waiting to be kissed awake. Sometime in the next ten years, perhaps her prince will come.

L.A., HOW DO I LOVE THEE? (UNDATED)

L.A., how do I love thee? Let me count the ways, or, perhaps, let me count one all-encompassing way.

Los Angeles as incubator of forlorn talents. Let me go back to 1934. Hand me my roller skates. With them I skated through life in Los Angeles when I was fourteen.

Seated at an Al Jolson radio broadcast, I was stunned when Jolson leaped off the stage and seized the roller skates off my lap. He jumped back onstage and started putting them on. I jumped after him and tore the skates from his hands. I then spun around, lifted my skates to the audience, and protested, "My transportation!"

Later that month I encountered W. C. Fields in front of Paramount Studios. I skated over to him and asked for his autograph. He handed it back to me and cried, "There you are, you little son of a bitch!"

And there I was, outside Paramount Studios, staring at the wall over which I hoped one day to climb to become part of motion pictures.

At that same time, I encountered George Burns in front of a theater in downtown L.A. where he and Gracie Allen broadcast their *Burns and Allen Show* every Wednesday night. In those days there were no audiences. I asked George to take me into the broadcast, and, not noticing, or pretending not to notice the roller skates under my arm, he took me and my friend Donald Harkins into the theater, and Burns and Allen performed their radio broadcast for an audience of two in an otherwise empty theater.

During the following weeks, I wrote and gave to George Burns some primitive radio scripts, and he praised them even though he secretly knew they were terrible. He pronounced me a genius and told me I had a great future as a writer.

In the following years, I stood on a street corner selling newspapers, and when friends passed by and asked me what I was doing, I said, "Becoming a writer." They said, "You don't look like one." I replied, "But I *feel* like one."

When I was nineteen, I went to confront the actress Larraine Day, who had put together a little theater group at the Mormon church. I wanted to write plays and act in them. Larraine Day looked at me with a cynical eye and was on the verge of turning me down when I cried, "You've got to let me in! I've told all my friends you would accept me!" She accepted me, and I ended up writing a musical with her and playing in that musical.

Over the years I continued writing, and in my twenties I wrote stories and sent them to Bill Spier, who directed and wrote and produced *Suspense Radio* for CBS. He invited me up to his house on Bellagio Road and never asked where I came from or where the stories had been published; they had been published in *Weird Tales* for a half cent a word. He accepted me for the quality of the stories, and I became a writer for *Suspense* in the following years.

Finally, with a single short story that John Huston read, "The Foghorn," I was offered a chance to write the screenplay of *Moby Dick*.

All of this, over a period of time,. with no one questioning where I'd come from or where I was going, nor did they notice the invisible roller skates on my shoes.

A day came when I went to the premiere of *Moby Dick* and noticed, standing in the rain outside the theater, two people who had once collected autographs with me outside Paramount Studios on that day when I met W. C. Fields. I ran over to them and introduced myself. They had long since forgotten the crazy kid who had roller-skated around Hollywood with them in 1934. When they asked me what I was doing at the premiere, I was totally embarrassed but finally admitted I had written the screenplay. In the crowd around my two old friends, there were twelve autograph collectors, and suddenly their hands reached out on the air with their autograph books. I signed them with tears in my eyes, knowing that at long last I had climbed over the wall carrying the roller skates under my arm.

At a banquet years later, I was giving an award to Steven Spielberg when I noticed George Burns over at a table in the corner of the Cocoanut Grove. I stopped the proceedings and said to the audience, "I've got to give my own award to George Burns, who treated me so kindly and told me that I was terrific when I wasn't back in 1934." When the program was over, George Burns ran up to me and shouted, "Was that you?! Was that you!? I remember you." We embraced for the first time in forty years.

I guess the answer to all this is that I was someone who skated through Hollywood with no money whatsoever but some ideas between my ears and wound up very late in the day with roller skates in hand and my memories of these people who accepted me without question, because the ambience of Hollywood in those days, and still in many places, was open and gratifying.

L.A., OUTTA THE WAY AND LET US HAPPEN! (2000)

Three images:

That general who leaped on his horse and rode off in all directions.

The inspired chicken who, placed on a rainbow plate, laid plaid eggs.

Ten million Angelenos marching to 10 million drummers, all different.

That's L.A.

New York? Ten million White Rabbits crying, I'm late, I'm late, for a very important date.

Paris? A big, beautiful nose that too often detects fish.

London? A larger nose, sending the fish back.

But L.A. now. L.A.?

The true center of the world. Inventor of most sport fashions for women with long lives and short skirts.

The absolute nexus of television. All TV films are born or born dead here.

The absolute San Andreas Fault line for films that crack the world.

And then there's our changeless weather, that endless summer toward which our whole continent surfs dreaming landfalls on Muscle Beach in one great jumble sale of sunburned limbs.

Our endless summer.

Oh, how they hate us for that!

They got us wrong long, long ago.

Describing L.A. as the laid-back, snooze-happy town.

Laid-back, no. Stand-aside, yes.

To let you pass, let you go, let you become.

It only pretends to be cool. I hate cool people. Next thing you know, they are cold. Soon after, they rent rooms at Forest Lawn. Not us.

We are in a state of becoming. If we persist, we go on becoming whatever in hell it is we want to be.

First off, and best, we don't believe in neighbors. Neighbors are a concept that, if you're not careful, fence you in. We are, in that way, truly western. The cowboy off his horse in Steinbeck's *Red Pony* faced with the Pacific, with nowhere to go.

Save that there *is*. We simply turn on our heel, spin slowly, to become ourselves. Our continental boundary is just turf. We don't have to accept its landfall palisades or its seeming run-out-of-space. We can simply stroll off through Subliminal Acres. Fancy talk? Maybe. But we wish to stay separate and ignore, if possible, those e-mail idiots trying to run up our noses and out our ears.

So that's it. Los Angeles is everything *you* want to be. Whatever you decide, L.A. becomes. It's going nowhere. *You* are.

Your engine drives the machine. The machine isn't laid-back, nor is it la-la-land-encrypted. It only *looks* that way. It's waiting for you to tromp the gas and hit and spark.

You want to thrive in the foothills, linger at the beach, carouse Boyle Heights, pretend a half-life in Beverly Hills? Do it.

The simple fact is, there is no Los Angeles. With luck, there never will be. Our prayer should ask that these eighty towns, these eighty oranges in search of a navel, never find it. The connective tissue that once fused jigsaw L.A., the big red Pacific Electric trains, have sunk in freeway dust. And the freeways?

Are mobbed with people aboard an attractive nuisance. Crammed with gas-buggy immigrants who each day must make up places to go because, mostly, they're going nowhere.

So listen up, stay off those no-destination freeways. Keep to the side streets, live your special life, cancel your *Variety* subscription with its foibles, fibs, lies, and disinformation.

Shoot off in any direction along this languid octopus's tentacles to find that the San Bernardino orange groves have not truly vanished but picked up their bright skirts and headed for the foothills, there to take root and drop fruit. Between freeway and orchards, find that mix of wineries and dairies that Got Milk? and One More for the Road California reds. Wade the Ventura surf or jump off a Torrey Pines cliff, whose citizens deny it, but, hey, it's all L.A.!

Stand in the center of the empty cement L.A. dry bed and sing:

> *Got to cross that river,*
> *Got to cross that hardbed river.*
> *There's no water in that river,*
> *But I'll walk upon that water*
> *'Cause the river's in my head!*

And so reach the far side and Mexico City Two to find a huge piñata that, whacked, will flood Broadway with Castilian and taco-brown complexions.

Ride Ventura Boulevard's Cornucopia Mile floodgates of restaurants, nail emporiums, and palmistry shops that outrun H. G. Wells's futures.

Or sand-surf Venice and its baroque rococo outré burlesque carnival sideshow geeks' half-lives. Where beauty itself, being rare, is the greatest show on Earth.

Survey your yards. There, by God, are the lawn-mower no-mads trimming grass and manicuring azaleas, *un*wetbacks from Guadalajara and El Paso; tall, not short, Oriental sumo wres-tlers who know how to thwart, tie, and twist a maple tree into a bushido box.

Laid-back? Hell, no. What appear to be immovable L.A. feasts may blossom as picnics. What seems a rootless statue is an idea inside a self-made chrysalis that may crack and let free a papillon or death's-head moth. Not an invalid trapped in a life of quiet desperation, but suffering serene inspirations in this adjunct to the U.S. Patent Office. Where some of the best twentieth-century ideas leaped forth as cripples and learned to walk, then run, by the Irving G. Thalberg Building or the Warner Bros. commissary. Where the Jews circled their tribal wagons and birthed Hollywood. Where Thomas Mann, Aldous Huxley, Igor Stravinsky, Christopher Isherwood, and Henry Miller, blown across the world by the winds of war, grabbed hold and grew beanstalks.

So here's to Los Angeles, diverse, multitudinous, going nowhere, arriving somewhere, a gigantic pinball machine with several million balls ricocheting off the future. May it never be integrated, may it never be described. With its tentacles snaking south to La Jolla, north to Santa Barbara, east to Palm Springs, west to Catalina, what a sprawl, what a roulette, what an Ohio-Iowa collision. It's Hello, I Must Be Going country. It's a last night I saw upon the stair, a super town that wasn't there, it wasn't there again today, my God, I wish it'd go away town. Not full of men running helter-skelter just to run helter-skelter. Laid-back? No, standing aside to let some other genius, torch-brained madman pass.

When François Truffaut, the talented French film director, first visited L.A. years ago, we ended the night on top of Mulholland Drive, where we showed him *our* City of Light, five hundred square miles of lights extending from sea to (almost) Salton Sea.

"See all those lights," I said. Six million lights, each representing an individual who doesn't have to join the pell-mell rush, who is not laid-back but merely considering the ganglion just under his heart, those nerve endings that know what it wants better than TV ads, better than your battered brain. Six million singles who don't have to "go fetch!" but turn in circles on their own Reebok deck shoes, watching the freeways fill with quasi New Yorkers while they quietly manifest themselves on off-paths and side streets, managing to get where they want to go ahead of the crowd.

L.A. My town. A town with no elbows, no hustles. Where you pick your neighbors, ten miles off, and ignore those across the fence if their shadow lies funny on the lawn.

A town with an ignorant subway that arrived at Hollywood and Vine recently. Folks wander up for a look-see, find nothing, turn, go back down, and try again some other year. A town of those endless summers with the ghosts of surfers nudging Malibu, daring the mud slide to hide them or the brush fire to torch, out beyond reach, not laid-back but upright, riding high. A town more *reale* than real and therefore a town worth dreaming in. A town where you can trade your tits and ass for a stroller and playpen and not mind the change.

And way up ahead in 2101 Millennium Third? In bungalow courts and multiplex flickers, new generations of mellow kids better educated at last, at last, mapless, chartless, just by going will arrive.

I would go there to that bee-loud glade, to Innisfree Two, California.

Finally, hark (as they once said) from all across the five hundred miles of the City of Light, L.A.

Can it be? It is!

The sound of 10 million people.

All marching . . .

To a Different Drummer.

L.A., WE *ARE* THE WORLD!:
A NEW-MILLENNIUM REVELATION (1989)

I have traveled to Paris, Rome, London, and Dublin. When I was there, did the natives ask about New York? Nope. Washington, D.C.? Chicago? San Francisco? No way.

What *did* the locals in Florence, Venice, and Madrid desire? California? Almost. Los Angeles? Closer. Hollywood? That's *it*. Hollywood!

To hell with the rest, beautiful and fascinating as they are. Tinseltown. With tons of tinsel beneath the tinsel.

Hollywood. Your town and mine. The hometown of all the Continental peoples. Yet when was the last time you truly looked? With the millennium on the fast track, isn't it time *we* did?

Not a political arena, architectural wonder, or science study hall. Underfoot, so close we cannot see ourselves, the most important city with the most important people in the world. Otherwise, why would tourists arrive in mobs?

Hollywood! With L.A. wrapped around the edges.

It's time for a quick look-see.

To see how we have failed our own image and to blueprint ways of salvaging our tenth-rate Champs-Elysées and our Elephants' Boneyard of Twilight Gods in much need of rebirth.

Commence with Hollywood and Vine. Probably as famous as Piccadilly, the Via Veneto, or Times Square.

Permit me to quote a one-minute TV spot I wrote last year:

FADE IN: Full sky. A Japanese jet shrieking from Tokyo to California. Sounds of cameras being loaded. Tourist voices gibbering.

"Oh, boy, oh, boy, Hollywood and Vine, can hardly wait, can hardly wait. Hollywood and Vine!"

The jet lands. More camera clicks as two hundred Japanese tourists leap out to stare at the hills. "Hollywood and Vine, Hollywood and Vine, oh, *boy*!"

In limos they race across town, yelling, "Can hardly wait! Vine! Hollywood!"

To burn rubber at the famed intersection.

Ten dozen Japanese leap out, beaming wildly. "Hollywood and Vine!"

They lift their cameras, stare, and give a last despairing cry: "Holy shee-it!"

One fast chorus of "Hooray for Hollywood!"

BLACK OUT.

For there *is* no Hollywood and Vine.

Let me walk you through the ruins of that impossible loss that might soon be a possibility regained.

Job One for January 1, 2001.

But Hollywood, you protest, isn't L.A. Like it or not, it *is*.

How do you revamp Hollywood and Vine so it looks like Hollywood and Vine? With all its famous shops and cafés vanished, how can the intersection stand tall, resplendent, and symbolic of a terrific past but a diminishing future?

It needs something to shock us with metaphor, perhaps not beautiful but at least redolent of 1900, 1939, 1980, and New Year's A.D. 2020.

Erase the Eiffel Tower, diminish Paris. Destroy Big Ben, London capsizes. No Taj Mahal? Forget India.

We can't fling up a tower, a clock, or a tomb. So . . . ?

Let me suggest a small model.

At the corner of Beverly Drive and Olympic in Beverly Hills stands a bronze monument, a twenty-foot-tall film scroll up-flung to the sky. At its base, in bas-relief, stand vivid portraits of some of the stars who created Beverly Hills: Mary Pickford, Douglas Fairbanks, Tom Mix, Rudolph Valentino, Harold Lloyd, and Will Rogers.

What if we re-created a similar upthrust pylon at mid–Hollywood and Vine, but *fifty* feet tall, panoplied in gold, with the star bas-reliefs of others who created the Hollywood image? Make your own list. Judy Garland, Bob Hope, Cecil B. DeMille. A competition, perhaps, to recall the famous at the center of our lives, with the endlessly unwinding ribbon of film, lit as to make it seem endlessly in motion, rising, to vanish in the stars.

With that grand reel of film flung to unspool itself in the heavens, wouldn't the world's tourists, arriving, shout, "Yeah! Hollywood and Vine, by God. At long *last*! Hollywood and Vine!"

Still, that's not L.A. Yes, it is! You just don't want to admit it.

Flinching back from that monument, what *else* can save Hollywood?

Are we using its ruins creatively?

Consider . . .

Tour buses prowling its bleak avenues are hard-pressed to summon up some freshly laundered ghosts. Visitors from Kankakee, Birmingham, and Ossining peer out and snooze. Why?

On Gower Street south of Sunset lie the old Columbia Studios. The soundstages remain, leased by tennis pros and badminton stars. On the sides of the old buildings lie a dozen empty billboards, thirty by twenty feet in size. They have stayed empty since Marilyn Monroe went away.

Why not give the tour-bus riders a feast? Why not replaster those old billboards with wide-screen ads from our salad years?

As you pass Columbia, look! What do you see? Above one frame: "In this soundstage in 1932 was filmed *It Happened One Night*." On the billboard, giant-size Gable and Colbert, ripe for Academy Awards.

Next soundstage, next billboard: "In this building, 1937, was filmed *Lost Horizon*." There, godlike, an immense Ronald Colman in Shangri-la.

Your tour bus almost jerks to a halt. *Surprise!*

Moving on . . .

A mile south on Gower, at Melrose, is the old RKO Studios, devoured by Desilu, devoured in turn by Paramount. Similar soundstages with similar empty billboards.

Slow your tour bus:

"In this building, 1932, was filmed *King Kong*." There's Kong atop the Empire State Building with Fay!

"In this soundstage in 1935 was filmed *The Gay Divorcee*." And Fred and Ginger up high, forever dancing.

So? Gower from Sunset to Melrose is a hall of mirrors; flying down to Rio, hitchhiking across America, or floundering through Tibetan blizzards in an hour's excursion, wouldn't your tour-bus addicts stare and run rampant with delight? I say they would. I say they must and shall.

So much for Hollywood. Now consider the rest of restless L.A.

Some eighteen years ago, I was invited to the Dorothy Chandler Pavilion one day to address the topic how to make theater popular with the peasants. Twenty—count 'em, twenty—famous orators were invited. People like Tom Brokaw; Philip Johnson, America's preeminent architect; Judd Marmor, the bright head of USC's school of psychiatry; plus seventeen others! Each had three minutes to expound, explain, and conclude. Three minutes each!? For Philip Johnson? Brokaw? Marmor? Myself as keynoter? Hell, let's stuff *Moby Dick* in a sardine tin! Good grief, I cried, Philip Johnson should have the whole day! Tut! they said. Get *out* there!

I exploded. What an insult to these talents! I cried, and ripped the skin off the day's organizers.

You want to popularize theater with the masses? I said. Your ticket prices are outrageous. Cut 'em! Parking prices for cars below, too high, cut! The cost of dining upstairs? Cut, cut. Do this! I said, and the mobs will storm Bunker Hill eager for O'Neill, ripe for *Richard III*!

Mrs. Chandler, in the front row, was stunned, wide awake.

Finished with my diatribe, I then redesigned all of downtown L.A., starting with the Music Center.

Here we stand in these high battlements looking down at Mexico City Two, but no way to get there. Crossing Hope Street is dangerous. Under the street lies a porcelain path through men's conveniences, which is to say, where the homeless, night and day, water the daisies. But before we leave this high place, we must refurbish the open esplanade between the pavilion, the Ahmanson, and the Taper. Why not invite attendees to arrive an hour before performances. Place a hundred tables and chairs out among small food banquettes and bars, serve light refreshments and twilight drinks, make it a social stage rather than a stone quarry.

Then build a bridge over Hope Street so that pavilion visitors, music lovers, can amble down to that northern shore of Mexico. Once every half hour, have a tour guide mariachi sing a gaggle of the curious down to a Broadway freshly parqueted like Rio's shoreline and follow this mosaic riverbed all the way to Olympic Boulevard, amid new streetlights, new storefronts, new paint, new glass, Mexico City Two reborn first class, then turn about and follow the mosaic pathway to Third, turn, and collide with Little Tokyo. Everything afoot. Those arriving at Little Tokyo by car would stash them and walk on to Olvera Street and Chinatown. How, with vast traffic boulevards between? Build a bridge of music and light to soar from Little Tokyo to land your wild pedestrians in the Zocalo. Then through Olvera on a street of lanterns hurrying toward Chinatown, a path teeming with textures, colors, and curiosities. Pedestrian traffic *both* ways, making the grand circuit from chow mein to enchilada to sushi!

And all cars abandoned! No more tourists climbing in their cars to visit another country just two blocks away. Inevitably, instead of reparking, Dad rode the gang home. So General Lee's to La Golondrina to Kyoto and repeat. Crowds return downtown! Street gangs? Policed. Warned away!

I finished my tirade to a standing ovation and got the hell out, leaving Johnson, Marmor, and Brokaw to their midget three minutes. My rebuilt L.A. hit the morning headlines.

Was my big two-hearted river of mosaics ever laid? Was that bridge from the Music Center ever arced to connect upper Bunker to lower Guadalajara?

Five years later the pavilion folks finally laid out a few tables and chairs with food and liquor so that people could at last come chat at twilight, enjoy the heights, but shun Mexico a hill slope away.

Don't stop me. I've just begun!

Why, you ask, do you keep beating that dead horse?

Because L.A. isn't dead, just lying low till *we* wake up!

The future is Hollywood, the future is us, but we blush to acknowledge this as an insult.

Think again: People don't want White House tours but front-row seats at the Phantom's Stage Nine Universal Opera House.

They'll land atop the Empire State Building, but only if Kong is there.

They won't sleep overnight in Frisco but bed at the Bates Motel and ask Hitch to tuck them in.

They don't want politicians but royalty: Lassie, C3PO, the Cowardly Lion. *Them*, they trust.

Add it up, Hollywood and Vine, Gower Street, downtown L.A., the big two-hearted river road through Tokyo, Guadalajara, and Peking, and you have a possible twenty-first century L.A.

Hell, I yelled all this years ago. No one listened, dreamed, or built. Because I gave it all free? I should have charged half a mil for my two-bit city-plan philosophies. L.A. might have changed. Maybe.

What else?

When Century City was built thirty years ago, they showed me their plans. Won't work, I said. Will, they said. Won't! I said.

They opened and flopped. Coming back to me, they said, Will you give more advice?!

Read my lips, I said, two hundred open-air tables, nine hundred chairs for people-watching, thirty restaurants. The secret of shopping is *eating*! Twelve cinemas! A great bookstore! Go!

They finally built the "Marketplace" restaurants, added the tables and chairs, and *voilà*! Century City entertains ten thousand eating shoppers each week!

What can we learn from this?

More outdoor restaurants spread through our vast and as-yet-untouched territory!

What else?

Reopen the Brown Derby just south of Hollywood Boulevard. No, not the original but a smaller tea and cocktail dive with all those fabulous star caricatures plastering the walls. A brief hideout where tourists can reconsider the past.

Make sure that the Egyptian Theatre is finally renovated so that inch by inch, block by block, we reconquer a Hollywood that currently resembles downtown Hiroshima.

Tell everyone about Larchmont Boulevard. Cars hurtling by on Beverly Boulevard rarely glance and spot this quiet, small shoppers' delight. Shade trees, pleasant shop owners, nice clientele, great Christmas browsing. Does it need additions, perfecting? Look into it.

Does everyone know Farmers Market at Third and Fairfax? An open-air fruit-and-vegetable movable-feast mall that has outlasted three generations.

And finally, on New Year's Day, 2001, let us pour ten thousand tons of cement in our never-should-have-been-started, never-to-be-finished subway for final rites. For its concept was always insane, its possible fares preposterous. Even if it were finished and opened, no one could afford to use it. Everyone has forgotten the experiment of a few years ago when bus fares were reduced to a basic twenty-five cents and one hundred to two hundred thousand new customers showed up to ride. Think how many cars that yanked off of freeways! No sooner was the experiment shown to be successful than it was canceled.

So kill the subway and telephone Alweg Monorail to accept their offer, made thirty years ago, to erect twelve crosstown monorails free, gratis, if we let them run the traffic. I was there the afternoon our supervisors rejected that splendid offer and was thrown out of the meeting for making impolite noises.

For remember, subways are for cold climes—snow and sleets in dead-winter London, Moscow, or Toronto. This is Mediterranean L.A., for God's sake. Autumn, William Faulkner said, is when *one* leaf falls in Laurel Canyon. Monorails are for high, free, open-air spirits, our always fair weather. Subways are Forest Lawn extensions. Let's bury our dead MTA and get on with life.

There's more, but I've run out of space.

To recap:

New Year's Day, January 1, 2001, and a grand tour of the reshaped, revitalized, and reconceived L.A. as great as and greater than it ever was.

Starting at dawn, being led downhill by a touring mariachi onto the Hispanic pavements of a refreshed Broadway, circling through Little Tokyo and crossing the Light and Sound Bridge to Olvera and then by lantern-lit alley to Chinatown, where throngs, long lost, rearrive, and thence out to Gower to stare up at Claudette Colbert, Ronald Colman, and Clark Gable blazoned on the old Columbia walls, and heading back at sunset to gape at the most famous star corner in all the world.

And there in the center, an award to ourselves, handsomer than Emmy, more beautiful than Oscar, the golden film spiral that starts with robberies on speeding trains and treks to the stars, with clips of Garbo, Chaplin, and Rin Tin Tin in its thrust. Bright at noon, fiercely and permanently evanescent at midnight. A proper gathering ground for glad arrivals, happy departures.

There at the center of the intersection, our award to ourselves and the destiny we did not imagine but now inhabit. Can someone give it a name? Speak up.

HOLLYWOOD and VINE, oh, boy, yes. No more waiting.

HOLLYWOOD AND VINE!

DISNEYLAND, OR DISNEY'S DEMON FOR HAPPINESS (UNDATED)

Some fifty years ago, I took my daughters to a kiddyland not far from my house. I wandered through this small environment with a Ferris wheel forty feet tall, a haunted house you could zip through in sixty-five seconds, and a roller coaster only seven feet high. The whole operation was run by some outré people who looked strange, sounded stranger, and smelled funny.

Simultaneously, wandering through that small park was a man with a mustache and his kids. He departed from the experience wondering why in all of Los Angeles there was only one small area that played to the needs of parents and their children.

In his office he experimented with mockups of possible rides and environments, using the talents of his artist friends. Finished, he borrowed millions of dollars on an experiment that everyone predicted would fail. His dream was finally built and opened against the doubts of everyone in the country, and the name of this dream created by the man with the mustache, for his kids, was . . .

Disneyland.

In the years following, in the midst of doubts, Disney proved that he had been infected by a Demon for Happiness. Surrounded by so much negativity, so much doubt, and so many strange places that looked odd, sounded odder, and gave off a high odor, he created a place where people could go and come forth smiling.

He based his feelings on three things that he felt were lacking, which he wanted to supply. He wanted an environment of trees. Thousands of trees and bushes were not necessary, but he placed them in Disneyland anyway. What about fountains? Who needed them? But he stationed them in Disneyland anyway. Was there a real need for extra benches where people could sit and people-watch? He placed those things strategically.

Studying Disneyland, you suddenly realize how much the New York World's Fair in 1964 could have used his input to make that experience an easy and wonderful one for all those who attended.

Disney knew from the start that there are two kinds of people in the world: people who enjoy happiness and people who hate it.

I was reminded of a dinner I attended years ago in which when I finished I said, "That was a beautiful meal." Someone across from me said, "No, that was good." So there you have the two kinds of people, who accept or who are afraid of happiness. Disney was among the first to challenge the notion that we should be afraid of happiness. On the contrary, we must embrace and celebrate it!

My first experience at Disneyland, happily, was with Charles Laughton. He flew me over London at midnight so I could look down on Big Ben, and during the day Laughton boarded the Jungle Boat ride and became Captain Bligh, keelhauling people and shouting orders right and left.

At that time there were many articles in intellectual gazettes making fun of Disneyland. I wrote a letter to one of them saying, "If it's good enough for the great dramatic actor Charles Laughton it's good enough for me."

During one period in the late sixties, several people tried to set fire to Disneyland. These were those joyless people who suspected any happiness.

Simply recall the reaction of some New Yorkers to Disney's invasion of Times Square. There were predictions that he would ruin the city by making it too clean. What happened, of course, was that the Disney people improved Times Square, rebuilt one of the old theaters, and put on one of the most successful musicals in history, *The Lion King*.

Finally, then, it is quite obvious that Disneyland is a place for people from all over the world to come and bring their private Demons, those Demons that are not afraid of happiness, to allow them freedom and give them air.

I end with one final story. I was crossing Disneyland one afternoon some years ago, and walking toward me the other way I saw a small girl in a bright blue-and-white dress, with long golden hair. As she approached and stopped before me, I looked at her and said:

"Alice in Wonderland?"

She looked at me and said:

"Ray Bradbury?"

ESSAY SOURCES

"Vin Revivere or A Vintage Revisited" first appeared in the June 1991 issue of *Gourmet* under the title "Dandelion Wine Revisited"; copyright © 1991 by Ray Bradbury.

"How Something Wicked Came" first appeared as "A Brief Afterword" in *Something Wicked This Way Comes*, Avon Books, 1998; copyright © 1996 by Ray Bradbury.

"All's Well That Ends Well . . . or, Unhappily Ever After" first appeared in the March 21, 2003, issue of the *Times Daily*; copyright © 2003 by Ray Bradbury.

"Remembrance of Books Past" first appeared in the February 2, 2004, issue of the *Wall Street Journal*; © 2004 by Ray Bradbury.

"Predicting the Past, Remembering the Future" first appeared in the January 2001 issue of *Hemispheres*; copyright © 2001 by Ray Bradbury.

"Mars: Too Soon from the Cave, Too Far from the Stars" first appeared in the September 2000 issue of *Space Illustrated* as "Too Soon from the Cave"; copyright © 2000 by Ray Bradbury.

"Earthrise and Its Faces" first appeared in *Infinite Perspectives*, Princeton Architectural Press, 1999; copyright © 1999 by Ray Bradbury.

"Falling Upward, or Walking Backward to the Future" first appeared in the March 1999 issue of *Interior Expressions* as "Falling Upward"; copyright © 1999 by Ray Bradbury.

"Beyond Giverny" first appeared in the March 15, 1994, issue of *American Way*; copyright © 1994 by Ray Bradbury.

"More, Much More, by Corwin" first appeared in the July/August 1999 issue of *Westways* as "The Corwin Chronicles"; copyright © 1999 by Ray Bradbury.

"Because of the Wonderful Things He Does" first appeared in *Won-*

"L.A., Outta the Way and Let Us Happen!" first appeared in *Imagining Los Angeles*, Los Angeles Times Books, 2000; copyright © 2000 by Ray Bradbury.

"L.A., We *Are* the World!: A New-Millennium Revolution" first appeared in the January/February 1989 issue of *Westways* as "Celluloid City"; copyright © 1989 by Ray Bradbury.

PREVIOUSLY UNPUBLISHED

"My Demon, Not Afraid of Unhappiness"
"Lincoln's Doctor's Dog's Butterfly"
"The Whale, the Whim, and I"
"Mouser"
"Lord Russell and the Pipsqueak"
"A Milestone at Milestone's: Bonderchuk Remembered"
"The Hunchback, the Phantom, the Mummy, and Me"
"I'm Mad as Hell and I'm Not Going to Take It Anymore (The New Millennium, That Is)"
"The Rabbit Hole Lost and Found Book Shoppe"
"Queen of Angels, Not Quite Ready for Her Close-Up"
"L.A., How Do I Love Thee?"
"Disneyland, or Disney's Demon for Happiness"

BOOKS BY RAY BRADBURY

THE MARTIAN CHRONICLES
ISBN 0-380-97383-9 (hardcover)

FAHRENHEIT 451
ISBN 0-694-52627-4 (unabridged CD)
ISBN 0-694-52626-6
(unabridged cassette)

DANDELION WINE
ISBN 0-380-97726-5 (hardcover)

SOMETHING WICKED THIS WAY COMES
ISBN 0-380-97727-3 (hardcover)

DEATH IS A LONELY BUSINESS
ISBN 0-380-78965-5 (trade paperback)

A GRAVEYARD FOR LUNATICS
Another Tale of Two Cities
ISBN 0-380-81200-2 (trade paperback)

GREEN SHADOWS, WHITE WHALE
A Novel of Ray Bradbury's Adventures
Making Moby Dick with John Huston
in Ireland
ISBN 0-380-78966-3 (trade paperback)

FROM THE DUST RETURNED
ISBN 0-380-78961-2
(mass market paperback)
ISBN 0-694-52628-2
(unabridged cassette)

LET'S ALL KILL CONSTANCE
ISBN 0-06-056178-5
(mass market paperback)

THE ILLUSTRATED MAN
ISBN 0-380-97384-7 (hardcover)

A SOUND OF THUNDER AND OTHER STORIES
ISBN 0-06-078569-1 (trade paperback)

A MEDICINE FOR MELANCHOLY AND OTHER STORIES
ISBN 0-380-73086-3 (trade paperback)

THE OCTOBER COUNTRY
ISBN 0-380-97387-1 (hardcover)

I SING THE BODY ELECTRIC!
And Other Stories
ISBN 0-380-78962-0 (trade paperback)

QUICKER THAN THE EYE
ISBN 0-380-78959-0
(mass market paperback)

DRIVING BLIND
ISBN 0-380-78960-4
(mass market paperback)

ONE MORE FOR THE ROAD
ISBN 0-06-103203-4
(mass market paperback)
ISBN 0-06-008117-1
(unabridged cassette)

THE CAT'S PAJAMAS
Stories
ISBN 0-06-077733-8 (trade paperback)

BRADBURY STORIES
100 of His Most Celebrated Tales
ISBN 0-06-054488-0 (trade paperback)

AHMED AND THE OBLIVION MACHINES
A Fable
ISBN 0-380-97704-4 (hardcover)

BRADBURY SPEAKS
Too Soon from the Cave, Too Far
from the Stars
ISBN 0-06-058569-2 (trade paperback)

For more information about upcoming titles, visit www.harperperennial.com.

HARPER ● PERENNIAL